KU-315-238

The Nose That Nobody Picked

David Parkin

Copyright © 2016 David Parkin
Edited by Maxine Linnell
Illustrations by Amy Nicholson

The moral right of the author has been asserted.

Apart from any fair dealing for the purposes of research or private study,
or criticism or review, as permitted under the Copyright, Designs and Patents
Act 1988, this publication may only be reproduced, stored or transmitted, in
any form or by any means, with the prior permission in writing of the
publishers, or in the case of reprographic reproduction in accordance with
the terms of licences issued by the Copyright Licensing Agency. Enquiries
concerning reproduction outside those terms should be sent to the publishers.

Matador
9 Priory Business Park,
Wistow Road, Kibworth Beauchamp,
Leicestershire. LE8 0RX
Tel: (+44) 116 279 2299
Fax: (+44) 116 279 2277
Email: books@troubador.co.uk
Web: www.troubador.co.uk/matador

ISBN 978 1785890 062

British Library Cataloguing in Publication Data.
A catalogue record for this book is available from the British Library.

Printed and bound in the UK by TJ International, Padstow, Cornwall
Typeset in 12pt Adobe Garamond Pro by Troubador Publishing Ltd, Leicester, UK

Matador is an imprint of Troubador Publishing Ltd

For the children in my life.
For Isla, Joe
and for Evie.

Spring

spring

The Sneeze

Early one sparkling spring morning, the Postlethwaites' garden echoed with cries of agony and terror. Past Mrs Postlethwaite's nice neat lawn, beyond the row of trees, within an overgrown jungle of plants and flowers ... something screamed.

A tangle of vines and branches shook as the terrible shriek ripped through the air. "Aaaaaarrrrrgggghhhh!"

A boy's head appeared above a bush and looked around. He wiped the sweat from his forehead and then plunged back into the undergrowth.

Another cry shattered the silence.

Christopher Postlethwaite was weeding.

Christopher didn't mind weeds in general; they were all welcome to grow on his patch of land … except one.

"Thistles," he muttered, and yanked one of the spiky plants from the ground. The ten-year-old let out a blood-curdling yell as he threw it over his shoulder. "AAAAiiiiiieeeeeee!"

Although he hated thistles, Christopher enjoyed weeding them. He liked to imagine they cried out in pain as he wrenched them from the earth. It made him feel better about all the times they prickled his hands.

"Yeeeeeaaaaaghhhh!" he roared as the last thistle flew through the air. He took off his gloves and surveyed his patch of garden.

Christopher was particularly proud of his ornamental displays. Vicious-looking gnomes guarded the entrances to mysterious caves, toy soldiers slowly sank into dark and smelly swamps, and headless dolls with arms outstretched walked through the wilderness, like zombies stuck in an endless game of blind man's buff…

"Looking good and not a thistle left standing," he said. "Not bad for a morning's work!"

Then a very strange thing happened.

He heard a sneeze.

"Hello?" he said. "Is anyone there?"

It was a busy spring morning with all the usual activity. The birds were building their nests and the spiders were hanging their webs, all about him the garden was preparing for another year, but Christopher couldn't see anything that might have sneezed.

"Must be imagining things…" He brushed himself down and looked at the pile of thistles at his feet. "Right!" he said as he scooped up the weeds. "It's the compost heap for you lot!"

"Aaaashooo!"

Another sneeze. Christopher dropped the thistles and glared around. "Now I *definitely* heard that!" He stood perfectly still and listened very carefully.

A faint sound was coming from the other side of his garden. "What *is* that?" He took a few steps toward the noise, then froze.

A patch of tall grass was moving in a very odd way, and something – or *someone* – was wheezing. He had to strain to hear it: a heavy panting sound. With every gasp and huff the grass trembled.

Christopher felt his heartbeat quicken.

"Probably just a sick badger … maybe a fox…" he said, but reached down for a gardening fork all the same. There was something about the wheezing that wasn't quite right. It didn't sound like any animal he knew. He held out the fork in front of him and took five small steps towards the rustling greenery.

"It's okay," Christopher called. "You can come out. I won't hurt you."

The back of his legs began to tremble as he watched the wheezing grass. He steadied himself, then peered into the foliage. "Right, let's have a look and…"

"AAAAASSSSHHHOOOOO!"

Another sneeze, the loudest yet, burst from the

grass, blowing dandelion seeds and a wet sticky spray into Christopher's face.

"Yeugh!" Blinded by the goo and seeds, Christopher stumbled backwards into a bucket, then forwards onto a rake, which flew up and thwacked him on the nose, which pitched him backwards again. He cluttered over his rockery and fell onto his bottom with a heavy thump.

The rustling stopped.

The garden fell silent.

Christopher rubbed the gunk from his eyes, felt the bump on his forehead and squinted angrily at the grass, which stood perfectly still.

"Time for a change of plan," he said as he scrambled onto his hands and knees. "Let's try this another way."

The breathing began again, but quieter this time: a sad sniffling sob. Christopher crawled catlike toward the noise. When he was as close as he dared, he reached out and carefully parted the tall grass.

Arnold, one of Christopher's gnomes, stood amongst the weeds and flowers. Christopher watched him intently.

If he wasn't mistaken, Arnold was moving ever so slightly. The gnome was wobbling, just a little, but wobbling none the less.

Also, Arnold looked *weird*.

There was something wrong with his face.

Christopher peered closer. "What's going on here?"

Although Arnold smiled on stiffly as always, he

looked different. Damply suckered to the middle of his face, between his two rosy cheeks, was a nose. A very big nose, speckled with ginger freckles. And it wasn't a nose made out of clay, like the rest of Arnold. This was a real nose, a proper human nose, made out of flesh and bone.

Christopher's jaw hit the floor.

The nose shivered slightly, and a steady flow of snot poured from its nostrils and dripped down Arnold's red shirt. Arnold grinned bravely on and stared blankly into the distance.

"This … this can't be real." Christopher glanced around. Maybe somebody was playing a trick on him.

The garden was empty.

"Where did you come from?" he asked.

The nose just sniffled and sneezed.

"You don't seem very well."

Christopher's head began to spin and his legs felt weak. "Let's just sit down for a minute and have a think about this…"

He clumsily cleared himself a space among the plants and flopped down onto a bed of dandelions. A fat bumblebee narrowly missed a squishing. It buzzed angrily into the air, but Christopher didn't notice. He just sat and stared.

There was a living nose, right in front of his eyes. He still couldn't believe it.

There was only one thing for it. He would have to touch it. If he touched it, he'd know if it was real.

He held out his hand and realized it was shaking. He took a few big gulps of air and waited until it was steady. Then in one quick movement he reached out and prodded the nose's right nostril.

It felt cold and damp, like a frog. The nose twitched and Christopher swiftly pulled back his hand.

"Yeugh … you feel like you've got a fever."

Christopher bit his lip and thought for a minute.

"I can't just leave you here," he said. "You're not going to last long. If the chill doesn't get you, something else will. A sparrowhawk lives a few gardens away … you'd be a very easy breakfast."

The nose just sighed and dribbled more snot down Arnold.

Christopher regarded the shivering, sorry-looking creature and decided he had no choice; he'd feel too guilty if he did nothing.

"Come on, let's take you somewhere warm … are you ready?" He cracked his knuckles, then added under his breath, "I'm not sure I am."

Christopher had picked up all sorts of slimy stuff before. He knew the best thing to do was not to think about it. He squeezed his eyes shut, held his breath and then lunged.

The nose came free from Arnold's face with a long, wet, sloppy, plop.

The Sniffling Pocket

Christopher slowly opened his eyes. The nose lay on his palm. Thick green bubbles popped from its nostrils.

"There..." he said, feeling quite unwell. "That wasn't so bad."

"Who're you talking to?"

Christopher whipped the nose into his pocket

and spun round. Standing right behind him was his younger sister Lauren.

"What have I told you about sneaking up on me?"

"I didn't sneak," said Lauren. "I just came out to see what you were doing."

"What does it look like I'm doing?"

Lauren straightened her glasses and gazed at Christopher with serious eyes. "I don't know, that's why I'm asking."

Christopher huffed. "I wasn't talking to anyone…"

"You *were* talking though," said Lauren. "Unless I'm hearing things."

"I was … I was talking … I was talking to my plants," said Christopher. "It helps them grow."

"Sun and water help them to grow," said Lauren slowly. "Talking doesn't do anything." She paused. "Unless your plants have ears."

Christopher looked at the smirk creeping across his sister's face, and felt a flash of anger. "What would you know about plants?"

"Probably about as much as you do!" replied Lauren, raising her voice to match his.

"Okay then," said Christopher. "What's the best way to pick up a nettle?"

"Explain photosynthesis," countered Lauren.

"Where would you plant a snapdragon?"

"Why did the tomato go red?"

Christopher floundered. "What?"

"Because it saw the salad dressing."

"What are you talking about?" said Christopher. Then he got the joke. "Oh really hilarious! Haven't you got anything better to do?"

Lauren looked into his eyes. "Come on Christopher, I was only teasing."

Christopher frowned at his sister. "Why can't you just leave me alone?"

There was a loud sniff. Christopher's pocket twitched.

"What have you got in there?" asked Lauren.

"Nothing," said Christopher, pushing past her.

"Not another mouse…"

"No really, it's nothing," said Christopher. He needed to get the nose inside, and think about what to do before telling anyone else about it. Especially his annoying sister.

"Where are you going?"

"Erm…" The nose sniffed again but louder this time. It sounded like it was building up to a sneeze.

"To the toilet," said Christopher. "I'm bursting for a wee!"

His walk turned into a run as the nose's huffs and puffs became quicker and more powerful, all the while rising in pitch. He sped over his mother's nice neat lawn and burst through the back door.

He dodged around the kitchen table and ran straight into his mum.

"What's the rush?" she said. "You nearly knocked me off my feet."

"Toilet!" blurted Christopher.

"Oh right." Mrs Postlethwaite sidestepped swiftly, and Christopher disappeared up the stairs. "Remember, put the seat down when you've finished!"

Christopher bounded along the landing, burst into the toilet and locked the door behind him.

"Just in time," he panted. Right on cue, the nose let rip with a loud, damp sneeze, deep inside his pocket.

Christopher felt the snot seep through the fabric and onto his skin. He cast a glance downwards and winced.

"This is going to be messy," he said. "Very messy."

What Do Noses Eat, Anyway?

Christopher made up a bed for the nose and placed it on his desk. He spent the rest of the afternoon staring at it where it lay, in a shoebox lined with thick football socks and cotton wool. The nose twitched its nostrils

and snuffled. In the last ten minutes its breathing had become deep and slow.

Christopher was sure it had fallen asleep.

"Do noses dream?" he whispered to himself as he rested his chin against his arms.

He still couldn't quite believe his eyes.

The oddest thing about the nose was its back. Christopher had never seen the back of a nose before, but he was pretty sure they didn't usually look like this one. Where the nose had stuck onto Arnold, where a normal nose would usually join a face, this one had countless tiny dark red suckers. When Christopher prodded them with a pen they weakly clung to the nib like sea urchins.

"This is all too strange."

All his life Christopher had always wanted something incredible to happen to him. He wanted to be the boy who discovered an alien in his shed, or stumbled upon the last living dinosaur.

But now he just felt numb. He didn't know where to begin.

He put his head to one side and squinted into the shoebox.

"You're just a little nose really," he said. "Alone and sick. Just a little nose…"

Christopher furrowed his brow. "I say little, but you're quite a big nose as noses go… but still, right now," He fluffed the cotton wool, "you seem very small … small and helpless."

The nose snorted in its sleep.

"I guess that makes you a big little nose. No, that's not quite right … you're a … little … *big* nose."

Christopher repeated the words louder; they had a nice ring to them.

"Little … Big … Nose…" A grin spread across his face. "That's what I'll call you … Little Big Nose…"

With that the nose snuffled awake and let rip with three short sharp sneezes.

"And you even recognise your name," laughed Christopher. "Brilliant!"

Encouraged, he decided that it was time for action.

Little Big Nose wasn't the first helpless creature that he had looked after. He had nursed back to health many baby frogs and small birds that had strayed too far from their ponds or nests.

A sick nose couldn't be that different.

"Right! Let's get you well again," he said, and held a hanky to the nose's chapped nostrils. "Blow!"

With a huge puff, Little Big Nose filled the hanky and more besides. Christopher looked down in horror and slowly spread his fingers. His hand looked like it belonged to some strange swamp creature. Green, slimy and webbed.

"That was pretty disgusting!" He grabbed a T-shirt and wiped off the goo. "But I suppose I'd better get used to it."

Christopher threw the snotty shirt over his shoulder and looked hard at the dribbling nose.

"Okay! Do you think you can manage some dinner?" He jumped to his feet. "What do noses eat anyway? My nose doesn't eat anything. But you have to be different. Everything that's alive needs food."

Christopher thought for a moment. What would he normally start with in this situation?

"Well, let's try some worms and see how we go."

Glasses Of Goo

Later that day, Christopher glumly sneaked out of the house carrying a tray of glasses all filled with thick, dark mucus. So far he had made no progress with the nose whatsoever. If anything, Little Big Nose was getting worse. He tried all sorts of things from his mum's cupboards, but couldn't get him to eat anything.

Christopher had held the nose in his hand, saying soothing words and catching the endless flow of snot in the various glasses. He filled up six. It had been a long day.

He slowly shut the back door behind him, wincing at the hinge's slow creek. It was early evening and a strange hush had fallen upon the garden. Christopher glanced at the full moon that hid behind a cloud, and a shiver whispered down his back. He decided the best thing to do with his collection of gunk was to pour it down the drain as quickly and quietly as possible.

"What you doing?" Christopher jumped and nearly dropped the tray. It was Lauren. She pushed her curly red hair out of her eyes and smiled at him.

"Oh, it's you," said Christopher edging around slightly, trying to hide the tray. "Creeping up on me again – what do you want?"

"Oh, not much," said Lauren. "Just finished my homework so I thought I'd pop out for some fresh air."

In the dusk sky a lone bat zigzagged overhead.

"You've spent even more time than usual hiding away," said Lauren casually as she watched the bat's dizzy display. "Locked up in your room…"

She turned to Christopher and narrowed her eyes. "Are you up to something?"

"Oh you know. Same as you … homework."

"Homework?" Lauren looked at him over her glasses. She was only eleven months younger than Christopher and was in the same year as him at school.

She liked it and always got top marks. Christopher didn't. She knew he only did homework if absolutely necessary. "What homework would that be then?"

"Erm…"

"The maths project about triangles or the history essay about the ancient Egyptians?"

"The Egyptians…" said Christopher. "The urm … the building of the stinx…"

Lauren laughed. "It's Sphinx not stinx! And besides, we're not doing the ancient Egyptians this term, I made that up. You haven't been doing homework at all, have you?"

"I've been busy," said Christopher trying to get past her whilst still hiding the tray.

"What have you got there?" Lauren stood on tiptoes to peep over his shoulder.

"Nothing. Go away."

"Yuk! It looks disgusting, whatever it is!"

Christopher stopped and thought for a moment. Lauren hated slimy, icky things … this might be fun.

"It's snot," he said, and proudly pulled the tray from behind his back.

"SNOT!" spluttered Lauren, stepping back. "Where did you get all that from?" Then she froze, and her eyes widened as another thought struck her. "What are you going to do with it?"

Christopher frowned and looked at the green mucus-filled glasses in front of him. He hadn't really thought this through. Showing her the goo had been fun for a moment, but now he had to explain it. He didn't want to tell her the truth; he liked having the secret of Little Big Nose all to himself.

"It's for my garden," he said in a flash of inspiration. "I've had a bit of a cold and I've been doing some experimenting. It turns out that snot is excellent for killing thistles."

Lauren stared at him blankly.

"So you collected all that snot to kill weeds?"

"Just thistles," said Christopher. "I don't mind the other weeds."

Lauren narrowed her eyes. Christopher met her gaze with a look of blank innocence. Lauren tilted her head to one side and raised an eyebrow. Christopher held his breath.

"Well, don't let me stop you," she said. "It's getting dark. Go on. Weed away."

"Good! Thank you very much," said Christopher. "I don't see what it's got to do with you anyway!"

Lauren watched him go with a confused look on her face. He really had changed over the last year. He used to like having her around but these days he spent nearly all his time on his own, either working on his garden or in his room.

She huffed with frustration. He was a puzzle she couldn't work out.

"Gardening with snot," she mumbled. "What next?"

In his garden Christopher looked at his tray of goo and then at a rather nasty looking thistle that had sprung up right in the middle of one of his ornamental displays. He peered back at the house, Lauren was still on the doorstep and he could tell she was watching him through the trees. He shrugged and began to tip the snot-filled glasses all over the weed. "Oh well, it might work, I suppose."

By the time he had finished, the thistle was well and truly covered. In the evening light Christopher thought it looked like a vicious space alien, spiky, green and slimy.

"IT CAME FROM ANOTHER PLANET TO DESTROY OUR GARDENS!" he boomed in an over-the-top movie voice. "ONLY ONE YOUNG BOY COULD STOP IT! THE THISTLE MONSTER FROM THE PLANET JUNIPER WOULD LEARN TO FEAR THE NAME…"

"Christopher Postlethwaite!" It was his mum calling him from the kitchen window. "Dinner's ready!"

Christopher looked the thistle right in the stalk and sneered: "I'll be back."

"Christopher!" His mum's call was sharper this time. "It'll get cold."

Then he was off, over his mother's nice neat lawn and through the back door, slamming it behind him.

Then there was silence…

High above, the clouds crept off into the darkness and the full moon shone down, drawing long dark shadows across the lawn and painting everything silver.

In the middle of Christopher's garden the thistle started to sparkle gently.

Slowly, steadily, each spiky leaf twinkled under the moon's gaze. Then the slimy thistle began to glow. As the moon continued to shine, its strange light glittered and grew.

The trees swayed silver in the breeze, the shadows slid from the bushes and an incredible green light engulfed the garden.

A Horrible Dark Day

A month of spring sunshine and showers went mostly
unnoticed by Christopher. He only really left his room
for school or on Saturdays, when he went on long bike
rides or walks in the country. He spent most of his time

making sure the nose was comfortable, trying to tempt him with different food and reading to him.

Christopher had never read so much. They were getting through about three books a week. It was the one thing that seemed to soothe the nose. His breathing would become less ragged, and he would sometimes pull himself up onto his nostrils and sit quietly, like an attentive child. But these occasions became less frequent as Little Big Nose's condition worsened. He spent days without moving, became very pale and the tiny suckers on his back turned from a dark red to a deathly grey.

One damp Sunday Christopher finally gave up all hope of Little Big Nose ever getting better. It was a horrible dark day. Christopher was feeling particularly miserable as he read *Pinocchio* to the trembling nose. He mumbled the words halfheartedly as he slowly munched a sandwich.

"Okay, that's the end of that chapter," said Christopher, trying to sound excited. "Next chapter tomorrow. It's a good one, I can tell you. I think he gets eaten by a whale!"

Christopher smiled weakly at the pale nose. "That crazy wooden kid!"

He gazed at Little Big Nose sadly and put some music on. Christopher was just thinking that the nose probably wouldn't last the day when a small piece of lettuce fell from his sandwich and landed in Little Big Nose's box.

The nose's nostrils flared instantly and began to sniff the air furiously.

Christopher jumped. "You all right?"

Little Big Nose sucked in a huge breath and then blew it out again. He panted lightly for a second and then drew up another nostril-full and exhaled noisily.

"Hey, it's okay," said Christopher. "Just slow down."

But the panting became faster and louder, so much so that Little Big Nose jerked violently from side to side.

As the slow seconds passed, Christopher watched helplessly as Little Big Nose puffed and spluttered and trembled and twitched. Panic crept up his neck as the shoebox shook, and the nose's gasps for air became high-pitched wheezes.

"Take it easy," he said desperately. "What's wrong?"

Little Big Nose pitched frantically to and fro, his breathing fast and desperate. Just when Christopher thought he had no more puff in him, he let rip an ear-piercing sneeze that propelled him high off the ground. The nose flipped through the air once, twice, and then landed, splat, upright on his damp nostrils.

"Bless *you!*" shouted Christopher's mum up the stairs.

"Thank you!" called Christopher.

He looked back to the nose.

A moment passed as Little Big Nose seemed to compose himself.

Then he began to wriggle.

He inched forward.

A short pause.

25

Another bit of wriggling and nostril flaring moved Little Big Nose further across his box.

Christopher let out an excited laugh. "You can walk … I mean crawl, sort of…"

The nose stopped in front of the lettuce. He opened his nostrils wide and inhaled.

"I don't believe it!" shouted Christopher as he watched Little Big Nose suck up the piece of lettuce like a vacuum cleaner.

"You eat lettuce?"

Christopher was amazed. He could just about stand lettuce in a sandwich, but it had never occurred to him that anyone or anything would like it on its own. He jumped to his feet.

"Well, I suppose someone's got to. Okay, wait there. I'll be right back!"

Christopher ran downstairs and flung open the door to the larder. He hurriedly tucked a lettuce under one arm and a cabbage under the other. His mum entered the kitchen wondering what all the commotion was about. "What are you doing?"

"Getting lettuce," said Christopher. "Oh, and a cabbage."

"Yes, I can see that, but why?"

Christopher paused. He had to think quick.

"You know, Mum, I'm worried about my diet," he said. "I'm a growing boy and I need to make sure I get the proper amount of minerals and vitamins."

"So you're going to eat a cabbage and a lettuce?"

Christopher's mum looked doubtful. "Do you want anything else with that, maybe sugared sprouts for dessert?"

"No, this ought to do it." Christopher went to leave, but his mum folded her arms and gave him *the look*.

He was backed into a corner. There was nothing else for it. Christopher breathed in, closed his eyes and then took a large bite out of the cabbage.

His mother's eyes nearly popped out of her head.

"Mmm…" he cringed. "Not only good for you, but tasty too!"

He ran upstairs, burst into his room and spat noisily into the bin.

"Eurgh!" He held up the vegetables to Little Big Nose. "This is disgusting! You like this?"

Little Big Nose's nostrils twitched instantly.

"Clearly you do!" Christopher ripped off a leaf, rolled it into a long thin tube and offered it to the hungry nose.

With a mighty suck, the entire leaf disappeared up Little Big Nose's left nostril.

"Wow, you *are* hungry!" Christopher tore off another leaf. "Would you like some more?"

Little Big Nose let out two strange-sounding sighs.

Christopher stopped dead in his tracks. He rose slowly to his feet, pulled the windows closed and turned off his music.

Very carefully he leant right into the shoebox and lowered his ear to the nose. "What was that?" he said.

The two breathy sighs came again, but this time Christopher could just make them out.

"*Yes ... please.*"

Little Big Nose followed his first whispery words with another three husky snuffs.

"*Chris ... to ... pher.*"

The Animals
Of The Garden

Although Little Big Nose was on the road to recovery, Christopher's work was far from done. He was busier than before.

Whenever the nose awoke from his fevered sleep,

Christopher would be there with lettuce and cabbage and various other bits of greenery.

The nose also requested pond water to drink, so Christopher often scurried back and forth to his garden with beakers and cups. The nose slurped the water up through a straw, and then slipped back into his troubled slumber.

Little Big Nose only spoke in fits and starts, usually short sentences, thanking Christopher, or asking him to read. He occasionally muttered while he slept, but the words made no sense.

On the fourth day he woke up with a chirpy sneeze. It was a cool evening. Christopher looked out of his window, and saw that his favourite birds had returned for the summer.

The nose's nostrils flared. "The swallows are here..." he said from his shoebox.

Christopher noticed that he was a healthy pink and his freckles had never looked so ginger. "How are you feeling?"

"Not too bad," said the nose. "I would very much like some fresh air."

Christopher gently picked him up and placed him on the windowsill. He looked at him with quiet awe.

"I still don't understand how you can talk ... and how you can understand me."

"As you read to me, Christopher, I listened and I learnt."

Little Big Nose's voice was a gentle whisper. Christopher had to make sure *he* listened hard.

"And I would still like to know how Pinocchio ends…"

"You learnt English just like that?" Christopher was amazed. "I've been doing French for a year now … and I still haven't got a clue!"

"I have always tried hard at languages," said the nose. "It can be very difficult to get to know someone if you can't understand a word they say."

"You can speak other languages too?"

"I'm proud to say that I can. I speak mole, sparrow, frog…"

"You can talk to animals! That's amazing!" Christopher sat on the edge of the bed and stared at Little Big Nose intensely. "I'd love to be able to do that! You really are incredible."

Little Big Nose's pale nostrils flushed a deep pink. It was the first time Christopher had seen a nose blush.

"We are all incredible … in our own way…"

"So can you speak to every sort of animal?"

"Not at all," said the nose. "For a start, a lot of creatures don't want to talk. Trying to strike up a conversation with a toad is a very tricky business."

Christopher felt a giddy rush of excitement. He was being given a glimpse into a strange and secret world that no other person had ever seen.

He wanted to know everything.

"What are badgers like?" It was the first question that jumped into his head.

"Lovely creatures. True gentle beasts. But ever so shy…"

"Snails?"

"Snails … snails are, in many ways, the dimmest slimers that you will ever meet." The nose paused for a moment and snuffled thoughtfully. "But you can't blame them. Any animal that carries its home on its back is always going to be a little simple. To never have to think about where you've been or where you are going may be very convenient … but it is terribly bad for the brain."

"Tell me more!"

So Little Big Nose told Christopher all about the garden and the animals that lived there. He told him about the birds, who always seemed to be in a rush, silly, noisy creatures who never stopped to think, and about the foxes who passed silently in the night singing ancient songs about their freedom, and about the giggling newts and the babbling bluebottles, and about the chubby caterpillars who spent their whole lives looking forward to the few crazy days they spent in the sunshine, transformed into beautiful butterflies.

Christopher sat on the edge of his bed, enchanted.

"So who are your favourites? What's the best creature in the garden?"

"Slugs," replied Little Big Nose instantly. "Slugs are

by far the most wise, kind and noble beasts you will ever meet."

He paused for a moment before adding, "But maybe I am a little biased."

"How come?"

"Because my mother was a slug…"

Christopher was just about to ask how a nose could have slugs for parents when *his* mother shouted from the hall.

"Christopher Postlethwaite! Bedtime!"

Christopher quickly lifted Little Big Nose off the windowsill and placed him in his shoebox.

"Hold tight. I want to hear more about these slugs." He slid the box under the bed just as the door swung open.

"Pyjamas … Now!" declared his mum.

Christopher opened his mouth to protest.

"You've already been up half an hour longer than usual."

Christopher huffed and grumpily got ready for bed.

His mum tucked him in and kissed him on the forehead. A tiny smile played upon her lips.

"Did you enjoy your cabbage supper?"

"Most nutritious," replied Christopher very seriously.

"Next time … let me make you a salad."

"Will do."

"Goodnight then." His mum stood up and ruffled his hair. "My strange little man."

Christopher waited until the door had closed and he was sure his mum was back downstairs in front of the TV.

He reached under his bed and slid out the shoebox.

"So … did your slug mum tuck you in at night?"

But Little Big Nose was already fast asleep. He was snuggled in amongst the cotton wool and was snoring gently.

The Glowing Bush

The next morning, Christopher strode out onto a fresh blanket of dew.

Little Big Nose poked his nostrils from Christopher's coat pocket. "Spring," he snorted. "Maybe my favourite season. All the wonderful new smells. The grass, the trees, the blossom."

Christopher walked Little Big Nose around his patch of land and told him about his gardening techniques.

"Basically, I let anything grow," he said and glanced disapprovingly over his shoulder at his mum's nice neat lawn. "I like a bit of a jumble ... I mean ... I think it's wrong to cut your grass all the time and have perfect square hedges. Nature is meant to be wild ... not neat and tidy."

Christopher thought for a moment as he tried to find the right words. "It's like seeing lions at the zoo," he said eventually. "It doesn't seem right somehow."

"So your garden is like a wild lion!"

"Exactly!" Christopher pointed out various sections. "I've got all sorts in here. Roses, leeks, tulips, poison ivy ... I did have a Venus Fly Trap once, but ... she couldn't cope with the English winter."

He looked around the jumble of leaves, branches, vines and blossom. "The only plants I don't let grow are thistles!" He told Little Big Nose about the screaming game he liked to play when weeding them.

"It sounds like your garden gives you a lot of pleasure."

"And we haven't got to the best bits yet!" Christopher leapt into the chaos and began to point out his various ornamental displays: the swamp of no return, the baby frog playground, the dolls' graveyard...

"I think that not only are you a very good gardener," said Little Big Nose. "You are also a fine artist."

"An artist." Christopher felt a bit embarrassed. "I've never thought of it like that."

"I think your work with gnomes shows particular promise."

"That reminds me!" Christopher reached down into a large grassy section. "This is Arnold!" Christopher held the gnome in front of Little Big Nose. "Do you remember him?"

"I most certainly do," said the nose. "And I would like to offer my sincerest apologies to your gnomey friend."

Although Arnold smiled his usual smile, he refused to look at the nose. As always, he stared resolutely into the distance.

"Don't mind him," said Christopher with a smirk. "He doesn't talk much."

Christopher placed Arnold back in his usual spot and took Little Big Nose from his pocket. He wrapped him in a sock and placed him on a large rock. Christopher pulled up the stool he kept in his garden and sat opposite, looking at Little Big Nose with intense curiosity.

"So … Little Big Nose," he began slowly. "Last night, maybe I didn't hear right, but I'm sure you told me that your mother was a slug."

"I believe I did Christopher, yes," replied Little Big Nose slowly.

"What's the story, if you don't mind me asking?" said Christopher jiggling his knees.

For a moment more, Little Big Nose said nothing. Then he snorted out a hearty laugh.

"Of course I don't mind!" he said and wriggled about in his sock, making himself comfortable. "What better time to talk of beginnings, than on a beautiful spring day!"

Christopher sat forward and listened intently to the nose's wheezy whisperings.

"My story begins with a full moon. A while ago, long before I can remember, my mother sat all alone under the light of a marvellous moon."

It was the voice Little Big Nose had used the night before while talking about all the creatures that lived in the garden. It was one of the best sounds Christopher had ever heard. It drew you in ever so gently and then painted incredible pictures inside your head.

"My mother said it was the most wonderful night she had ever seen. Thousands of stars freckled the sky and the fat yellow moon seemed bigger and closer somehow, as if it were hanging just beyond the clouds."

"I love full moons," said Christopher.

"So do slugs," replied Little Big Nose. "And all other creatures, now I think of it. Maybe it's the one thing that all beasties agree on: that a full moon is truly a very magical thing."

"There's just something about a full moon that makes you feel really…" Christopher searched for the right words. "Really … *alive*."

"For a human you are a most perceptive character," said the nose.

Christopher smiled shyly.

"Anyway, on with the story ... so there was my mother ... crawling along, enchanted by the night's spectacle. She crept for hours, looking at the sky and taking in the smells of the evening, lost in her thoughts. Eventually she realised, however, that she had travelled a little *too* far and had no idea where she was."

"Was she scared?"

"Not at all. She was a slug, remember. Here's a little riddle for you: why is a slug never lost?"

Christopher thought hard for a moment.

"Because of their trails!" he shouted, feeling very pleased with himself.

"Precisely," replied the nose. "Wherever a slug wanders in the whole wide world, there is always a shining silver path just behind them, ready to lead them all the way home."

"That must be very handy!"

"Yes, indeed it is," said Little Big Nose. "My mother was just turning around to trace *her* trail when she saw the most unusual thing ... a glowing bush."

"Glowing?" Christopher looked doubtful. "She really saw a glowing bush?"

"Although this story is true, it does not mean that all of it happened," said the nose. "My mother, like all good storytellers, was prone to exaggeration. And anyway, it wasn't the bush that was glowing."

"What was then?"

"I was," replied the nose. "My mother said that when she looked into the branches there I was, covered in green glowing goo."

"You were pretty gooey when I met you," grinned Christopher. "But you weren't glowing!"

"Apparently I was an incredible but sad sight. I was small and pale and I sniffled and snuffled. My mother said she had never seen a beastie look so alone."

"So she took you in?"

"Yes, she did," said Little Big Nose. "She adopted me as a slimer of her own and I grew up as a slug ... as part of the herd."

"Didn't you stick out?" said Christopher. "I mean ... wasn't it odd, being the only nose?"

"I thought I was a slug for many years."

"But surely you must have noticed something was different."

"Not at all. In many ways I'm just like a slug. I trundle along slowly. I sometimes leave behind me a glistening trail, just as they do. I was brought up exactly the same as all the other baby slimers: on a healthy mix of riddles, philosophy and greenery."

"So that's why you like cabbage and stuff?"

"Yes, and thank you by the way for that delicious meal last night," said Little Big Nose politely. "I always knew I was not my mother's birth child, but I had no reason to think that I wasn't a slug."

"So how did you find out?" asked Christopher.

"That you weren't a slug, I mean. It must have been a bit of a shock."

Little Big Nose fell silent.

After a long pause he said quietly, "That, Christopher, is another story entirely. And one better left for another day."

"You don't have to tell me at all if you don't want to," said Christopher. "I understand."

"There's an old slug saying," replied the nose solemnly. "Given time … a sad story will tell itself."

"Okay…" said Christopher, not really understanding but eager to change the subject. He jumped to his feet and was just about to continue his tour of the garden when he felt something prickle his leg.

"OW!"

He looked down and there was the thistle that he had poured Little Big Nose's snot over a few weeks ago.

"So it doesn't work as weed killer…"

"I beg your pardon?"

Christopher laughed to himself. "Oh never mind … it's a long story, and I'm not as good at telling them as you are."

He reached down, grabbed the thistle and yanked.

"AAAAARRRRGGGGGHHHHH!" The cry echoed around the trees and bushes sending birds flapping into the air.

"That really is a gut-wrenching thistle scream you've developed there," said Little Big Nose.

But Christopher didn't reply.

41

"What is it?" said the nose.

"That wasn't me…" said Christopher in a whisper. "It wasn't me that made that horrible sound."

He looked around the garden nervously.

"And if it wasn't me, what was it?"

Little Big Nose sniffed the air. "I can't smell anything out of the ordinary."

Christopher looked down at the thistle in his hand. He was sure it twitched a little.

"Strange…" he said. "Very strange."

The Fantastic
Plastic Surgeon

The next day, Christopher was watching his favourite nature programme on TV when he noticed an advert on the back page of his mum's newspaper.

In big bold letters the advert asked, "DO YOU HAVE A BIG NOSE COVERED IN UNSIGHTLY FRECKLES?"

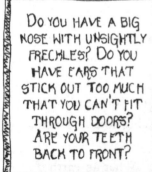

DO YOU HAVE A BIG NOSE WITH UNSIGHTLY FRECKLES? DO YOU HAVE EARS THAT STICK OUT TOO MUCH THAT YOU CAN'T FIT THROUGH DOORS? ARE YOUR TEETH BACK TO FRONT?

IF SO, WHY NOT CALL DOCTOR SKINNER? THE FANTASTIC PLASTIC SURGEON.

Christopher got up from the sofa to have a closer look; the advert went on…

"DO YOU HAVE EARS THAT STICK OUT SO MUCH THAT YOU CAN'T FIT THROUGH DOORS?

ARE YOUR TEETH BACK TO FRONT?"

By now Christopher was practically sitting on his mum's lap. His mum frowned at him over the paper. Christopher read on.

"IF SO, WHY NOT CALL DOCTOR SKINNER? THE FANTASTIC PLASTIC SURGEON.

IF YOU'RE LOOKING FOR A NEW FACE THEN HE'S YOUR MAN!"

"Perfect!" shouted Christopher, jumping to his feet and running from the room. He fetched a pair of scissors from the kitchen, burst through the door and snatched the paper away from her.

"What are you doing?" cried Mrs Postlethwaite as Christopher began to cut out a large square from the back page. "I was reading that!"

"You can have it back in a minute. I'm just cutting out an advert."

"What advert?"

Christopher showed his mum the square of paper. She frowned through her glasses, "A big nose … Doctor Skinner … teeth back to front?"

She looked up at Christopher. "What an earth do you want this for?"

"Urm … homework!"

"Well, that makes a nice change."

"Yeah, we have to write about what we want to do when we grow up." Christopher smirked to himself. He was getting rather good at telling fibs. "And I thought I might quite like to be a plastic surgeon."

His mum screwed up her face. "Really?"

Christopher nodded cheerfully, "Yep!"

"Right… " She rolled her eyes. "Well, there you go." She handed Christopher back the advert. "But wait until I've finished reading the paper before you start cutting it to pieces in future."

"Okay!"

"And another thing!"

"YES," said Christopher impatiently, skipping from one foot to the other.

"I think it's lovely that you want to pursue a career in medicine, completely out of the blue, but lovely all the same. But wouldn't you rather be a regular surgeon? It's just my opinion but I don't trust plastic surgeons."

"Whatever you say!" cried Christopher as he ran from the room.

His mum watched him go and then returned to her paper.

"Doctor Skinner indeed," she muttered. "Sounds like a villain to me."

SUMMER

Doctor Skinner's Mansion

The weekend came, and Christopher and Little Big Nose had breakfast before anyone in the house was awake.

Earlier that week Christopher had shown Little Big Nose the plastic surgeon's advert. The nose had seemed unsure at first and had gone for a trundle around the garden for a think.

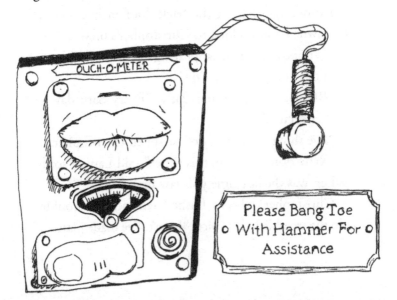

When Christopher found him, sitting on Arnold's hat, his mind was made up.

"I realised some time ago that I am a nose, for better or for worse," he said. "And if I'm a nose, then I should jolly well try to be one!"

So that Saturday morning, Christopher pumped up the tyres on his bike and placed the nose in his shoebox.

"It might get a bit bumpy," he warned. "Can you hang on to something?"

"Easy," replied Little Big Nose and with a squelch, he used his damp suckers to hold tight to the cardboard. "I'm ready."

Christopher grinned at the nose and slid the lid over the box. As he placed it in his rucksack he looked around at the bright greens and blues of summer.

"Good day for a bike ride..." he said breezily. Then he glanced back at the house and a frown fell across his face. "And I'm not hanging around here all day."

Lauren appeared at the back door in her nightie. She yawned and nodded to Christopher's bicycle.

"I suppose you're disappearing again..."

"I'm going on a bike ride."

"Right..." said Lauren flatly. "Every Saturday it's another excuse."

"I've things I need to do," snapped Christopher.

"Why don't you stay this time?" said Lauren softly. "When was the last time you saw him?"

Christopher's cheeks flushed red, and he couldn't help the tremble in his voice. "I can't. I've made plans..."

Lauren reached forward and tentatively took his hand.

"Come on Chris ... he really misses you."

"Lauren ... don't hold my hand!" scowled Christopher. Lauren let go and Christopher jumped on his bike.

"What have I told you about that?" he said. "We're not little kids anymore."

"You're going to have to see him sooner or later."

"Got to go now," said Christopher as he pushed his feet into the pedals. "Tell Mum I'll be back for tea!"

"Christopher..." Lauren called after him, but he was already half way down the drive. She watched him cycle up the hill and disappear around a corner. Then, for a while, she just watched the empty road.

Doctor Skinner's mansion seemed very posh to Christopher. It looked more like a small castle. As he pushed his bike down the long driveway he looked up. Steeples, turrets and towers jutted into the sky. Christopher glanced around at the gardens and decided they were a bit boring.

What this place really needs, he thought, is a moat.

When he arrived at the large front door, he was confused to find that there was no doorbell or knocker. But there was an odd metal box. Attached to the box was a mouth. Stranger still, just below the mouth, connected by wires and cable, was a toe. Below them both hung a hammer that dangled from the wall by a chain. Next to this was a sign that read: "Please bang toe with hammer for assistance".

Christopher inspected the strange contraption. The toe and the mouth looked incredibly realistic.

"Can't be real though," said Christopher as he picked up the hammer. "Must be some kind of plastic surgeon's joke." He banged the toe as hard as he could.

"OW!" screamed the mouth robotically.

"Just a minute!" shouted a voice. Christopher heard someone running downstairs and then the various clicks and clunks of locks and bolts. The door swished open and there stood Doctor Skinner.

The doctor was a shocking sight.

He was very, very tall. He had six fingers on each hand and his mouth looked huge, like it had too many teeth.

"Yes?" said Doctor Skinner, looking Christopher up and down. "I'm sorry, but whatever it is I'm not interested!"

Christopher said nothing and just stood there, flabbergasted.

"Are you all right? What is it? Cat got your tongue? I can make you a new one … for a price!" Doctor Skinner laughed at his little joke.

"You've got twelve fingers," said Christopher. It was the only thing he could think of.

"Yes … well spotted. Makes playing the piano a lot easier!"

"And you're very, very tall," said Christopher, still shocked silly.

"Extra knees," said the doctor in a hushed voice and winked at Christopher.

"OW!"

Christopher jumped.

It was the mouth on the metal box.

"OW! OW! OW!" it chanted.

"Blasted thing!" growled Doctor Skinner. "Look, just move out of the way for a second ... stupid contraption..."

The doctor bundled Christopher inside and stepped out onto the porch to investigate. The front door slammed shut. Christopher glanced around nervously; he hadn't meant to enter the mansion. He knew his mum wouldn't be happy if she found out he'd been knocking on strangers' doors. But Doctor Skinner seemed harmless enough, a little eccentric maybe, but harmless.

Then he heard the doctor dealing with his machine: a mix of thuds, mechanical cries and Doctor Skinner muttering to himself...

"Confounded piece of junk..."

THUD!

"OW!"

"...why doesn't anything work for longer than a few days?"

CLUNK!

"OW ... OW!"

"Stop whining, you useless..."

"OW ... OW... OW!"

"Right, you asked for it!"

There was a particularly loud KURTHUNK,

a crash as the metal box hit the floor and a lot of stamping.

"OW … OW … OW … OOOOOooooowwww…"

The mechanical voice trailed off and then was silent.

The front door opened and Doctor Skinner stood there looking dishevelled. The metal box lay in pieces at his feet. He stared up at Christopher as if surprised.

"Oh yes, you!" He reached into his pocket. "Look I haven't got much change … I don't know why you lot have to bother good people like me…"

"I don't want money."

"I bet you do. What is it then? Are you selling cookies or something?"

"No…" said Christopher. "I came to see you. I was hoping you might be able to help me."

"You came to see me?" Doctor Skinner seemed taken aback. "No-one comes to visit me. Not out of working hours anyway."

Christopher felt a bit awkward and shuffled his feet.

"In that case," said the doctor, grabbing Christopher's hand. "Do come in, come on!"

Before Christopher could say a word, the excited doctor was pulling him up a winding stair.

"I'll show you my laboratory! Prepare to be amazed!"

Christopher panted up the last set of stairs.

"Bit of a climb, I'm afraid," said Doctor Skinner. "But the view's worth it."

The doctor proudly opened the door.

For the second time that day, Christopher was speechless. The laboratory was high up in one of the mansion's turrets. Instead of a roof, the sun shone down through a huge glass dome that hung over the strange room. Christopher shielded his eyes and looked around.

One side of the room was engulfed by technology. Computer terminals hummed and beeped. Monitors crackled, and lots of strange machines that Christopher had never seen before buzzed with flashing lights and clunky mechanical noises.

"And these," declared Doctor Skinner, gesturing to the other side of the room, "are my specimens!"

Hundreds of jars of all different shapes and sizes stood upon rows and rows of shelves. Each one held a dark blue liquid and was labeled.

Christopher walked closer.

"I don't believe it," he said.

Ears, eyeballs, feet, noses, teeth, mouths, fingers, belly buttons and lots of other bits and bobs floated inside the glass jars.

"Pretty fantastic eh?"

"Erm … yeah." Christopher felt his stomach turn. "Really … fantastic."

"Aren't they just?"

"Where did you get them from?" asked Christopher, not sure if he wanted to know the answer.

"I make them." The doctor glared closely at his specimens. "And a very tricky procedure it is too. It's all about the ingredients, you see. You have to get the mix exactly right, otherwise it doesn't work at all. Just making one single eyelash is more complicated than you could ever imagine."

"So what do you do with them?" Christopher stared into a jar. An eyeball gazed lifelessly back. He took a few steps away from the shelves. "Do you use them for your plastic surgery?"

"Some yes ... but most I use for my own private experimentation."

"Experimentation?"

"Well firstly, there are my own personal improvements." The Doctor wiggled his twelve fingers at Christopher and grinned. "Secondly, are my *devices* ... which are my real passion."

Doctor Skinner spun away from his specimens and turned to Christopher.

"Plastic surgery ... although very good for bringing in the money, was never really a passion for me."

He fixed Christopher with a serious look. "And its so important to have a passion ... don't you agree?"

"Yes ... very important."

"My work," announced the doctor, "is the most important thing to happen to this world since the invention of the wheel! What did you think of the doorbell?"

Christopher struggled to find the right words. "Very ... unusual!"

"It's a prototype of course, still a few teething problems."

Then all of a sudden, out of nowhere, Doctor Skinner burst into giggles.

"Teething problems!" He cried. "Because it's a mouth … Oh dear … that's priceless … hee hee … teething problems… Heavens to Betsy … Sometimes I crack myself up…"

Christopher watched in awkward silence and tried to smile.

Doctor Skinner wiped a tear from his eyes, chortled a little more and then was deadly serious.

"My work, you see, brings together two very different things."

He pointed to his computer bank, "Technology" then turned to his specimens, "and the body. I call it Techbodylogy!"

Doctor Skinner glared at Christopher with a twinkle in his eye.

"Would you like to see some?"

Scuttler and Funky Feet

The thing darted across the floor and disappeared behind a computer terminal.

"Did you see it?" asked Doctor Skinner. "He's a nippy little fella!"

Christopher slowly sat on the swivel chair in the centre of the room.

"Not really…" He lifted his feet off the floor. "What is it? A spider?"

"Close," said the doctor. "But not quite right."

He fiddled with the large remote control in his hands. "Hang on a sec. I still haven't quite got the knack of this."

A finger appeared from behind the terminal, probing the air, as if checking the coast was clear. It was followed by another three fingers and then a thumb.

"I am proud to present…" said the doctor, "the incredible SCUTTLER!"

The thing did indeed scuttle across the floor. It scampered over to Christopher and stopped dead, right at his feet. Christopher yelped and clutched his knees under his chin.

And there it was: a remote control hand. Half flesh, half machine. An electronic box with flashing lights and antennas imbedded in its wrist.

"Now for the really clever bit!" said Doctor Skinner and flipped a switch.

There was a beep, an electrical whir and then, out the top of the hand, an eye blinked open and stared at Christopher.

"Is it friendly?"

"It's as friendly as whoever's got the controls," said Doctor Skinner as he handed them to Christopher. "Why not have a go?"

Christopher took the heavy remote.

"Look, there you are!" The doctor pointed to a tiny

monitor on the controls. Christopher looked down at the screen and saw himself as seen by Scuttler.

"So that's what I look like when I'm terrified," he tried to joke.

"It's cutting-edge stuff," said Doctor Skinner, taking no notice. "The computer in the hand transmits what the eye sees straight back to this remote."

The doctor snatched the controls back off Christopher and began to fiddle with the levers. Scuttler rose to its fingertips and then scampered away into a corner.

"Probably the most marvellous thing you have ever seen … right?" shouted the doctor as he disappeared into a closet.

"Probably the weirdest thing I have ever seen," muttered Christopher.

"Prepare to be doubly amazed!" Doctor Skinner burst back into the room, carrying another odd-looking machine. He placed the contraption in the middle of the laboratory. "Take a look at this gadget!"

This machine was considerably larger than Scuttler. Half of it was a very ordinary-looking record player with a few extra knobs and dials. The other half, however, was a hairy pair of legs. They stood underneath the record player like legs to a table.

"Being a genius, I don't really have time for socialising," said the doctor wistfully. "So life can sometimes be a very lonely affair."

He jumped back into the closet and reappeared clutching a record.

"But occasionally we geniuses like to have a little fun as well." He glanced over the record and placed it onto the turntable. "Hmmmm ... some jazz I think..."

Doctor Skinner grinned at Christopher.

"No-one to dance with?" he said as the music began to play. "Then why not try the incredible Funky Feet!"

The song started with a laidback beat, a double bass and a playful trumpet. The legs of the machine responded casually, a knee bent in time and a foot tapped to the rhythm.

Doctor Skinner clicked his fingers and grinned. "Cool daddy-o..."

There was a roll of drums, a blast of horns and the song exploded into a swirling swinging mix of beats and screaming saxophones.

Funky Feet jumped into life and flew across the laboratory, in a twirling display of high kicks and knee swivels.

Doctor Skinner clapped his hands in delight as the device jigged and jived around the specimen jars and machinery.

"Look at it go!"

By this point Christopher was feeling very uneasy indeed. Although the doctor's devices were incredible, they were also very creepy. And there was something about the strange doctor and his constantly changing moods that Christopher didn't trust.

"Erm … Doctor Skinner …"

But the doctor wasn't listening. He was watching Funky Feet and swaying to the music.

The jazz tune built to a crescendo, Funky Feet leapt into the air, clicked its heels and then landed with a heavy thud. The record skipped.

Doctor Skinner's face fell.

The skip in the record caused the legs to twitch and kick … which caused the record to skip again.

Doctor Skinner's cheeks turned a dark crimson as he watched Funky Feet turn from a debonair dancing device into a malfunctioning machine of mayhem.

The legs flung themselves in different directions, attempting a ridiculous kind of breakdance – which made the record skip – so they spun on one knee, while doing the highland fling with the other – which made the record skip again. The legs swayed and spasmed and twitched and twirled, and all the while the needle jumped from one spot to another, from one song to the next.

The doctor's eyes bulged as he watched the machine bang and crash around the room, jumping and kicking like crazy.

Christopher watched with a sense of déjà vu. For some reason, the out of control Funky Feet reminded him of how his mum danced at weddings. Doctor Skinner's huge fists clenched white with rage.

"Blasted thing!" he bellowed and threw himself upon the device.

Specimen bottles smashed, monitors cracked and Christopher watched wide-eyed as Doctor Skinner angrily wrestled Funky Feet to the floor.

"Confounded useless bowlegged rubbish!" One of Doctor Skinner's big hands grabbed at a foot as the other tore at wires, knobs and dials. "The only time I have a visitor and you have to spoil it all!" The record smashed and the legs flayed and fell limp.

Doctor Skinner stood up, flushed with anger, clutching half a broken record in one hand and a clump of leg hair in the other.

Then, for a whole minute he stood staring into nothing, his face a deep purple, his eyes bulging.

"Doctor Skinner?" said Christopher eventually. "Are you okay?"

The doctor blinked and looked at Christopher. He shook his head as if waking from a dream, then glanced around his laboratory.

"Right … sorry about that…" He ran his twelve fingers through his thinning hair. "Sometimes I get a bit carried away."

The doctor noticed the broken record he was still clutching in his hand. He gently placed it upon his desk and tried to smile. "What was it you wanted to ask me, anyway?"

Christopher had seen enough.

"Oh nothing…" he said, getting up.

"Come on, don't be shy."

"I had something to show you," said Christopher,

edging toward the door. "But it doesn't seem important anymore."

"How intriguing," said Doctor Skinner, a look of excitement dancing across his face. "It's in the bag, isn't it?"

"Well, yes," said Christopher. "But I really should be going…"

"Oh, don't be such a tease!" Doctor Skinner snatched Christopher's rucksack and delved inside.

Christopher watched helplessly as he whipped off the lid and upended the contents of the shoebox on to the floor. Cotton wool scattered everywhere and then with a small splat, a terrified Little Big Nose hit the floor.

"Oh." The look of excitement fell from the doctor's face. "That old thing."

"What?" said Christopher.

Doctor Skinner looked at Little Big Nose with a sneer.

"It's very nice of you to return it but I threw it out years ago. You can keep it."

The Nose Is Mine!

Christopher picked up Little Big Nose and clutched him to his chest.

"You made him?"

"Of course," said Doctor Skinner. He peered at the nose. "It was some time ago now. I was just learning, but it's definitely one of mine." He pointed to the damp little suckers that lined the nose's back.

"See, it's got my trademark BURPs!"

"Burps?"

"Biological Utility Retention Puckers. To think, some plastic surgeons are still *sewing* bits and bobs onto people."

"So your specimens can stick *themselves* onto patients?"

Doctor Skinner snorted. "Well, it's a bit more complex than that, but you've got the right idea…"

He walked over to his desk and grabbed a small book.

"If I'm not mistaken, that particular specimen was made quite a few years ago. Let's have a look in one of my old diaries … I think this is the right one," he said, flipping through the pages. "Yes, here we are … it was when I was experimenting with noses that made their own mucus."

He looked up from the book. "There I was working on it, when the damn thing exploded and covered us both in snot."

Doctor Skinner cast the diary aside. "I never did work out how to make a stable mucus gland. All the noses I make now are dry. It's not as realistic, but what can you do?"

"So what happened?" Christopher felt Little Big Nose begin to sniffle and tremble in his hands.

"I was *very* annoyed." Doctor Skinner frowned and stroked his chin. "I *think* I threw it out the window … you wouldn't guess it but I do have a little bit of a temper."

Christopher decided it was time to go.

"Right," he said. "I think I should head home now because my mum…"

"AAAACCCCHHHHOOOO!"

Christopher looked down at Little Big Nose and then back at the wide-eyed doctor.

"What was that?" whispered Skinner

"A sneeze," said Christopher, feeling like he was stating the obvious.

"A SNEEZE … how could it SNEEZE?"

"Well… " Christopher walked to the door. "He does that when he's nervous … *anyway* got to go now, thanks for your time!"

"STOP RIGHT THERE!"

Christopher froze in his tracks and looked round at the doctor, who stared at him wildly. "Is that nose alive?"

Christopher nodded.

"But this is incredible," said Skinner, never once taking his eyes from Little Big Nose. "A living specimen! I … created … a living nose."

Then once again, Doctor Skinner's mood changed. He was suddenly very composed and serious.

"As I said, thanks for returning the specimen." He held out a hand to Christopher. "Now if I could just have it back. I will pay you handsomely for this kind deed."

"But you said you didn't want him," said Christopher.

"But that's before I knew he was ALIVE," said Doctor Skinner, moving closer. "This is an incredible thing that has happened. I will need to do some experiments on the specimen…"

"Experiments?"

"There'll have to be a dissection, of course."

"Dissection…" Christopher knew what the word meant, it meant putting Little Big Nose to sleep and sharp knives. "You can't cut him up, he's a living thing!"

Doctor Skinner lunged forward and grabbed Christopher by the shoulders.

"I think you'll find I can do whatever I want…" he growled. "I made him! He belongs to me!"

"I most certainly do NOT!" snorted Little Big Nose.

"He can talk as well!" Doctor Skinner looked down at the nose in amazement.

Christopher seized his chance. "Yes, he can! And he doesn't want anything to do with you!" He kicked Doctor Skinner hard in one of his six knees, ran through the door and began to jump down the stairs.

"Come here!" yelled Skinner.

Christopher didn't look back. He flew down the stairs as fast as he could. He heard the doctor clattering after him. Christopher fell into the hallway and began to frantically unlock the front door. There were several bolts and locks, and his hands shook as he turned keys and fiddled with latches.

"Come back here!" the doctor cried from the

stairwell. The last bolt clunked open and Christopher burst through the door and out onto the drive.

He dragged his bike off the gravel and was just about to jump on it when he felt something clamp firmly around his ankle.

SCUTTLER...

The hand had a strong grip. Christopher watched, frozen with fear as it slowly crawled up his leg.

The eye on Scuttler's back opened and peered at him with cold robotic malevolence. The fingers tightened around his knee.

In an instant, pain flooded through Christopher's leg. He pushed and slapped at the machine, but Scuttler was too powerful, its grasp tighter than any human hand.

One by one Scuttler's fingers began to crush his knee. Christopher fell to the floor in agony.

He looked up at Doctor Skinner, who stood at the doorway with the remote control in his hands.

"Please ... please stop!"

"You didn't think you'd get away that easily." The Doctor chuckled and walked over to Christopher.

"I asked nicely," he said. "Now I'm just going to take what's mine."

"AAAAACCCCHHHHHOOOOO!"

With a huge sneeze, Little Big Nose leapt into action. He flew through the air and landed, with a wet splat, on Scuttler.

"What's going on?" said Skinner.

The nose began to huff and puff and snivel and sneeze. Christopher looked down and saw Little Big Nose blow out of his nostrils the biggest, greenest ball of slimy goo he had ever seen. There was a high pitched fizzing sound as the snot squelched and slimed all over the hand's computer implant.

Scuttler froze as the snot dripped into its circuitry. With a sudden spasm it released its grip and fell paralyzed to the floor.

"Why you little…" the doctor made a lunge for the nose.

Christopher gasped with relief, grabbed Little Big Nose just in time and hobbled to his feet.

"You're not going anywhere," said the Doctor, blocking his path.

"Yes I am," said Christopher as he lowered his head. "Through your legs!"

And with that he ran between the doctor's many knees, pulled his bike from the gravel and jumped on the seat.

"No! Wait!" Skinner spun on his heels, but Christopher was already off and down the driveway in a cloud of dust.

"The nose is mine!" he screamed. "I'll find you! I'LL FIND YOU!"

Christopher slipped the bike up a gear and pedalled away as fast as he could.

Full Moon

Mrs Postlethwaite pulled the bandage tight over Christopher's knee.

"Ow," yelped Christopher grumpily.

"Come on," she said as she wrapped the fabric in on itself. "It can't hurt that much." She plucked the safety pin from her teeth and secured the bandage.

"There … that ought to hold the swelling." She glanced up at her son. "Exactly how tall was this tree you were climbing?"

"Just average size."

"Really? Well, be more careful next time." She stood up and put her hands on her hips. "It's just you and me for tea tonight. Your sister's going to eat with your dad."

Christopher frowned and looked down at his bandaged leg.

"So I tell you what," said Mrs Postlethwaite. "You decide what's on the menu. Anything you want." She made a big display of performing an elaborate curtsey. "Whatever the young master of the house wants for his evening supper. Your wish is my command!"

Christopher tried not to, but he couldn't help smiling.

"Pizza?"

"As you wish." His mum bowed and then grovelled her way to the fridge.

"I'm sure we've got one in here somewhere," she called as she rummaged through the freezer drawers. "Yes here we go. Deep pan ok?"

"My favourite."

"By the way," said Mrs Postlethwaite as she slid the pizza into the oven. "Your father was asking after you today."

Immediately the smile fell from Christopher's face. Mrs Postlethwaite sat on the chair next to him.

"Don't look like that. I'm not having a go," she said gently. "It's just that every Saturday you disappear, or make some excuse not to see him."

"But I'd planned today. I couldn't just…"

"Christopher," his mum put her hand to his cheek. "I know this last year hasn't been easy."

"Mum…"

"But you know, just because your dad and I don't really get on any more, it doesn't mean you and him can't be friends."

Christopher stared into his lap.

"Christopher?"

"Can I camp in the garden tonight?"

"What?" This wasn't the answer Mrs Postlethwaite was expecting. "Well, yes of course but do you think…"

"Thanks." He got up from the table. "I think I'd better get the tent ready. Can I have the pizza later tonight when I've got everything set up?"

"Yes, if you want, but…"

"I'd better get busy before it gets too dark." Christopher quietly left the table and then ran up to his bedroom, slamming the door a lot harder than he meant to.

Christopher was driving in the last tent peg when Lauren ambled into the garden. He quickly popped Little Big Nose into his pocket.

"Just stay in there and be quiet, okay? It's only Lauren." He squinted through the dusk. "What's that she carrying?"

Christopher strolled over to his sister. As he got closer he could see that she was unfolding a tripod, planting its legs firmly onto the lawn and adjusting them until they were evenly spaced and sturdy.

"What's that for?" he asked.

"This!" said Lauren, producing an old telescope, which she then screwed into place on top of the tripod. "Thought I'd try it out tonight, on the full moon."

She looked through the telescope's eyepiece and began searching the sky.

Christopher felt a pang of jealousy, "Where'd you get that?"

Lauren looked up from the telescope and straight into her brother's eyes.

"Dad gave it to me … to us. He said we could share it. He found it when he was clearing out the attic of his new house." Lauren bent her head back to the eyepiece. "You haven't even seen Dad's new house have you?"

"I've been busy…"

"Of course you have," she said. "We went to the aquarium today, you'd have loved it."

"Really?"

"Yep, they've got a tiger shark now." Lauren frowned. "I can't see anything through this thing.

"It's because you haven't got your glasses on … here … let me." Christopher stepped over and took the telescope.

It took a while, changing the old implement's various focuses, but when the full moon came into view it was a staggering sight.

Christopher had looked at the moon often enough, but to see it close up was amazing.

Dark craters and vast mountain ranges covered

its surface. He'd often thought it was beautiful, but now he understood that it was more than that. It was a distant land with undiscovered caves and valleys. A whole other world, shining in the sky for all to see, but still unreachable and mysterious.

"WOW."

Lauren nudged him in the ribs, "Come on, let me have a go."

She took the telescope and looked into the night.

"It's incredible isn't it?" she said. "No wonder people used to worship it."

"Like who?"

"All sorts … Pagans, Aztecs, American Indians."

"Right … of course." Christopher rolled his eyes. "How do you know all this stuff?"

"I read…" said Lauren drolly. "You know, witches and druids still worship the moon today."

"Sounds to me like you've been reading too many kids' books."

"Not those sort of wizards." Lauren looked up from the telescope. "Real ones … modern witches and druids. You know … old people with long hair and sandals."

"You think Aunty Sally is a witch?"

Lauren laughed. "Maybe…" She peered back through the eyepiece. "They believe the moon has magic powers. Some of them only plant their herbs and roots when it's a full moon. It's called moon gardening."

"Well, I've never heard of it."

"Perhaps you should give it a go."

Christopher was surprised. "I wouldn't have thought you'd have believed in that stuff."

"I wouldn't say I believed in it," said Lauren. "But the moon controls all the tides on the planet, helps moths to navigate and, well … loads of other stuff. Who's to say it doesn't affect other parts of nature that we don't know about?"

"Yeah, I suppose so…"

She straightened up and put her glasses back on. "And we all know how a full moon affects you."

Christopher folded his arms, "Oh yes … and how's that then?"

Lauren hunched her shoulders, stuck out her tongue and panted like a dog. Then she tilted her head back and howled.

Christopher waited until she had finished. "You're very funny," he said flatly.

"I know," said Lauren with a bright smile. "Why don't you have the telescope tonight? I'm going in."

Lauren skipped back to the house. "Besides, it's safer indoors. It won't be long before you start growling."

"If I *were* a werewolf," called Christopher. "You'd be first on the menu!"

Lauren barked at him and then disappeared inside.

Follow Your Trail

Later that night, Christopher and Little Big Nose lay on the grass by the tent, gazing up at a sky alive with stars.

Although it was a beautiful evening, Little Big Nose was quiet and seemed lost in a world of his own. Christopher wondered whether their scary experience with Doctor Skinner had upset him.

"It was pretty terrifying today huh?"

Little Big nose just huffed half-heartedly.

"You were great though," persisted Christopher. "A real hero!"

"As were you…" snuffled the nose quietly.

Christopher raised his head on his elbow and looked at his friend. "Little Big Nose … what's wrong?"

A moment passed as the nose thoughtfully sniffed the air. "Can I ask you something?" he said eventually.

"Of course…"

"But first, I'd like you to close your eyes…"

"Okay…"

"Now," said Little Big Nose. "What can you smell?"

Christopher was a little taken aback by the question, but he raised his nostrils to the cool night air and took in all the delicious smells of summer, the cut grass, the fresh green smell of the trees and leaves, the sweet scent of the flowers and the rich dark smell of a dying bonfire that gently puffed out its last breaths a few gardens away.

For a while they sat in silence, Christopher with his eyes shut and the nose resting by his side.

Finally Little Big Nose spoke: "You can open your eyes now."

Christopher opened his eyes, yawned and stretched.

"So … what could you smell?"

"Lots of things," said Christopher, a lazy smile on his lips. "The grass, the trees, my pond, which I think needs cleaning … and a bonfire."

"Not bad," said Little Big Nose. "But did you know that slugs have such a good sense of smell that they would be able to sniff out a hundred more things in the night air. They would, for example, be able to tell you what had been burnt on that bonfire, whether it had been old furniture or new green shoots, trimmed from a rose bush."

"That's incredible," said Christopher.

"It is indeed," agreed the nose. "Nights, like tonight are very special for slugs. On a summer's full moon, slug herds gather together. Each slug closes their eyes and they sit for a long time in silence, enjoying the quiet and stillness of the night, breathing in the cool air with its rich kaleidoscope of smells."

A light breeze tickled its way across the tent and set the trees whispering.

"Eventually the moon fades into sunlight of course, and then it's time for each herd to head its separate way." Little Big Nose's voice became sad and distant. "But before they leave, each slug will sniff the night's fading fragrance one last time and then utter the most famous of all slug sayings."

"What's that?" asked Christopher.

"The world is beautiful … even with your eyes closed." A watery tear dribbled from Little Big Nose's nostril. "I miss the herd," he said. "I miss my mother."

Now in the tent Christopher sat with Little Big Nose resting on his knee.

"It was a night like tonight when it happened…"

Christopher knew he was about to hear Little Big Nose's sad story and listened in respectful silence.

"It was a wonderful dusk. The birds sat in the trees singing their lullabies and pink clouds rolled their way across the darkening sky. Many slug herds were gathered, humming quietly in anticipation of the night's full moon."

Little Big Nose was silent for a moment, lost in the memory of that beautiful evening. "The last thing we expected to hear at such a peaceful time was the slug distress call."

"What's a slug distress call?" asked Christopher.

"The slug distress call is only to be used in times of the utmost peril," said Little Big Nose. "It can be a plea for help, or a warning."

A shiver ran through the nose. "As it turned out that day … it was both." He sniffled a small sob. "We all listened in horror as a distant thud silenced the cry."

"It's okay," said Christopher. "Take your time."

"We tried to crawl to hiding places, but of course we were far too slow. The thuds got louder and louder until the whole earth shook with them. An immense shadow fell all around. And then, standing over us, blocking out the setting sun, was a human."

"Oh no…" whispered Christopher.

"Hot white rocks fell from the sky, landing on each and every slug."

"Salt," said Christopher. "It dries slugs up … Little Big Nose … I'm so sorry."

"It's not your fault," said the nose. "There are good and bad within all creatures. Just as there are humans who scatter salt on defenceless slugs, there are humans who are as gentle and as kind as you are."

"Thank you," said Christopher feeling a little proud.

"I, being a nose, was not hurt of course. But at that point I still did not know what I was … so I looked around in confused horror as all the other slugs began to bubble and fizz. The rocks sank into their banks, burning into their flesh."

"How horrible."

"I trundled to my mother as fast as I could. She did not have long to live, but before she died she told me that I was a human nose. She said she had been meaning to tell me that very night."

Little Big Nose sniffed back another sob. "Then she told me some other things I shall never forget. She told me not to be ashamed of what I was. That I had been a good slug, but it was time to be a nose."

"But how?" said Christopher.

"She said that I must follow my trail. She said if I followed my trail I would find out where I am from. Who I am. *Why* I am… And then, just before she died, she said something I had heard a thousand times before."

Little Big Nose wept quietly for a moment and then continued. "She said to remember that she had found me on a full moon, and that a full moon's child is touched by magic."

"She was right, you know," said Christopher and gently patted Little Big Nose.

"And so I left and wandered for days, alone with my sorrow. I became terribly sad and ill. That's when

you found me, pathetically clinging to Arnold's face …
trying to be a nose."

"But you could be one yet … we can still find you
a face."

"But that's just it," said the nose. "I will never find
a home. I have followed my trail and know where I'm
from. And rather than being a unique creature full of
magic … I'm just an experiment that went wrong. A
mistake … made by a strange lonely, old man."

"You mustn't say that," said Christopher.

"My mother was wrong…" said Little Big Nose.
"I am not special. There is no mystery … there is no
magic."

As Christopher tried to comfort his friend, the full
moon shone down on the first tear that Little Big Nose
had shed, which still lay in the grass, just outside the
tent.

The moon's pale rays made the teardrop shine and
sparkle, like a tiny immaculate emerald.

I Must Have
That Nose!

Doctor Skinner sat in his laboratory, alone and angry. A single candle burned and the distant stars shone down. He stared furiously at the noses arranged on his desk. Rows and rows of them: a week's work. Fifty big noses and a hundred dribbling nostrils. All of them identical to Little Big Nose in every way ... except one. None of them were breathing.

"I don't understand it." Once again he snatched at his diary and inspected the page in question.

"This is it! I'm sure!" He read from the book. "'The mucus gland in The Triple D Hooter has proved unstable. Hurled nose from window in rage. Must learn to control temper.'"

Doctor Skinner grabbed one of the noses and threw it across the room.

"I used the same ingredients! I followed the same procedures!" He rose to his feet and stared at the army of hooters. "You are all exactly the same as the specimen the boy had!"

One of the noses flipped into the air, its nostrils exploding with slime.

"Right down to the malfunctioning mucus gland," added the doctor. "And yet, none of you … are alive!"

Doctor Skinner clutched at his thinning hair. "Anyone alive here?" He spun around, addressing the whole laboratory.

His specimens floated silently in their jars. The eyeballs watched blankly. The lips that had never spoken did not break their silence. They just smiled on and hung lifelessly in their blue liquid, like so many dead fish. Another nose jumped in an eruption of mucus.

Doctor Skinner peered around with bitter eyes. "No! No-one alive here. Just me … as usual."

He flew into a rage and swiped at the shelves with his huge gangly arms. Jars flew across the room and smashed, scattering glass, ears, hands, elbows and eyes.

The doctor, his face red, upended his desk and stamped angrily on each of the fifty noses as they rolled around the floor.

The last nose squished beneath his boot.

"Come on Skinner ... think!" He looked up through the glass roof at the crescent moon.

"I just need to find out what's missing. What ingredient have I left out? What's the difference between a dead nose and a living one?"

The doctor slumped at his desk and sighed. With a heavy hand he reached into a drawer and pulled out a locket. He flicked it open and ran a thin finger over the old picture inside.

"I want to make you proud," he said to the faded image of a frail-looking woman. "All I need is that ingredient. That's all it would take."

He closed his eyes and his brow furrowed deeply.

"If I just had that ingredient, Mother," he said slowly. "There's so much I could do."

He looked to the photo. "You understand that."

The doctor's fist clenched slowly around the locket.

"I need to know," he muttered through gritted teeth. "No matter the cost."

He snapped the locket shut and jumped to his feet.

"There's only one answer," he shouted. "I must have that nose. Whether the kid likes it or not!"

He walked over to the dancing candle flame, his eyes shining with fire.

"Just one dissection ... that's all it would take."

His hunched shadow grew huge against the laboratory walls.

"I must find out the nose's secret."

His finger and thumb slowly closed around the flame.

"When I get hold of that kid," he said as the candle hissed and died, "he's dead meat."

AUTUMN

AUTUMN

The Old Tree House

Christopher and Little Big Nose sat in an old tree house and looked out on the autumn sky. Leaves fell below them in spiralling showers of amber and brown, and the creatures of the forest either stocked their larders or flew away to warmer lands.

"Winter's coming," said Christopher. "I hate winter."

Little Big Nose sniffed the air. "There's definitely a chill on its way."

Christopher looked at his watch. Five o'clock and it was already getting dark. "Autumn's *nearly* as bad … because you know winter's just around the corner." He dropped a twig and watched it tumble toward the dead leaves that littered the forest floor. "Autumn always makes me sad."

"Its true that autumn comes before winter," said Little Big Nose. "But in my opinion it's also the most beautiful of all the seasons."

Christopher sighed and looked around. From the height of the tree house the forest lay in front of him like a giant patchwork quilt of green, red and bronze. Christopher had to agree that it was beautiful.

"But a little sad," conceded the nose. "It seems to me that the most beautiful things in life often have something a little sad about them."

Christopher stared into the sunset. "Goodbye, sunshine."

It had been a wonderful summer, with long golden days and late hazy evenings. Christopher and Little Big Nose had spent most of their time in Christopher's garden. After their experience with Doctor Skinner, they had forgotten about finding the nose a face. They were happy to enjoy each other's company and the wonderful weather. But now it was coming to an end.

"Who do you think built this tree house?" asked Little Big Nose.

"That's easy," replied Christopher and began to brush and blow the dust off one of the walls.

Scratched into the wood were the words: 'David's tree house'.

"Do you think he would mind us sitting in it?"

"Well, this place is *really* old," said Christopher. "I expect he's grown up by now."

"But he might still visit."

"I doubt it … grownups don't climb trees, they drive cars and go to work and stuff. I guess they don't have time…"

"But there's always time to climb a tree!"

Christopher frowned. "Yes, I suppose so … I think it's that they don't really *want* to climb trees anymore."

"It would appear to me that humans are very different from slugs," said Little Big Nose. "Slugs get *wiser* as they get older, whereas humans seem to do the exact opposite."

Christopher and Little Big Nose laughed, both of them unaware that somewhere in the branches above, something was listening.

An aerial slowly rose into the air.

The device was half machine, half ear, and every time Christopher talked, a red light flashed and an ear lobe twitched.

Far away in Doctor Skinner's laboratory, an antique radio set began to buzz loudly. The doctor, who had been enjoying an afternoon nap, jumped to his feet and blinked his eyes.

"What's going on?"

When he saw the buzzing radio set, a huge teethy smile spread across his face.

"I've found him!" The doctor jumped to his feet. "All my work hasn't been in vain!"

Doctor Skinner had spent the entire summer hiding mechanical ears and eyeballs all around town. He had put them in schools, playgrounds, sweet shops and pretty much anywhere you might find children (including tree-houses) all in an attempt to hunt out Christopher and Little Big Nose.

He twisted a large knob on the radio and turned the volume up. It crackled and whined, but soon Christopher's voice could be heard faintly through the static.

"I've got the little squirt!" said Skinner as he lowered his ears to the speakers. "Now ... what's he saying?"

"I've been thinking, Little Big Nose," said Christopher's voice. *"And maybe it's time we started trying to find you a face again."*

Doctor Skinner sneered. "Isn't that sweet..."

"So I tell you what ... we can go to the library tomorrow to see if there's any books about this sort of thing. There's bound to be. There are books about everything. Well ... that's what Lauren says anyway..."

"Going to the library, are we?" The doctor switched the radio off and giggled to himself. "Well, I might just be there tomorrow as well. Maybe I'll take out some books or maybe ... I'll just take the nose!"

Doctor Skinner skipped over to his specimens. He was in such a good mood he decided to treat himself.

"I'll just have the one. I deserve it for being such a clever doctor!"

He brought the eyeball up to his lips and sucked it into his mouth in one big slurp. His cheeks bulged as the eye squelched and burst.

"Mmmm … Delicious!" he said, as the thick white juice dribbled down his chin.

We Meet Again!

As a rule Christopher didn't really like libraries. He never understood why they had to be such quiet, serious places.

"I'm doing this for you," he said to Little Big Nose as he tucked him in his pocket. He tried his best to smile as he walked past the severe-looking lady at the counter.

When he got in among the shelves Christopher realized that he had no idea what he was looking

for, and wandered about for half an hour scratching his head. Eventually he found a thin book about the history of the moustache and decided to start with that.

He flopped down at a table and opened the book.

"So, you little twerp ... we meet again."

Christopher's blood ran cold. He slowly looked up. Doctor Skinner towered above him with his long arms folded.

"Hello, Doctor Skinner..." said Christopher. "Fancy meeting you here."

"Be quiet and listen..." The doctor pulled up a chair and spread his twelve fingers across the table. "Now, I'm going to make this very simple. The nose belongs to me. If you don't hand him over I will have to take him from you."

"I ... I haven't got him anymore," said Christopher. "He ran away ... to somewhere ... somewhere very far away from here."

"Don't lie to me, pipsqueak!" spat Doctor Skinner. "I know you've got him, and I'm willing to bet he's sitting in your pocket right now."

Doctor Skinner looked down at Christopher's coat pocket. It trembled slightly and a small sneeze came from inside.

"Come on..." said the doctor. "Just hand him over and we can go our separate ways ... and forget this ... unpleasantness."

Christopher glanced at the exits. There was no way past Doctor Skinner. He was cornered.

A long minute passed as Christopher sat at the table and thought.

Eventually he frowned, nodded to himself and then slowly reached into his pocket. Doctor Skinner's eyes lit up and a huge grin spread across his face, "You won't regret this."

Little Big Nose sniffled and shook in Christopher's hand.

"I'm sorry," said Christopher to the nose. "But what can I do?"

Doctor Skinner reached across the table. "You know it makes sense, kid."

But before the doctor could lay his hands on the nose, Christopher jumped to his feet.

"Let's hope this works!" he said, and held the nose up in front of his face.

"Little Big Nose … suck!" With a big slurp Little Big Nose used his BURPs to stick himself to the middle of Christopher's face, right over his friend's normal, smaller nose. Suddenly Christopher looked like a little boy with a very big nose. A very big nose speckled with ginger freckles.

"Dight, Doctor Dinner," said Christopher in a low, calm, if somewhat strange, voice. "If you want da dose your gonna daff do dake me as well. He's duck on really dight."

Doctor Skinner scowled and banged his fist on the table. A red-faced librarian looked up from his desk and glared in their direction.

"And if you dake me I'll kick and scream da douse down."

"Why you little…"

"Christopher?"

Doctor Skinner turned. Across the library was a girl with glasses and red hair.

"Christopher, what are you doing here?" asked Lauren. "Everything all right?"

Doctor Skinner looked around the library. The red-faced librarian was still watching him intently and people were frowning at him over their books. As he stood up he whispered in Christopher's ear, "I'll get that nose yet…"

The doctor looked at Lauren and a cold smile fell across his face.

"Well *Christopher*. It's been very nice to see you again. And who may I ask, is this?"

Lauren put on her polite voice. "I'm Lauren, Christopher's sister. I help out at the library on Sundays."

Christopher winced to himself. He'd forgotten that. If he'd remembered Lauren was going to be there, he never would have come.

"Charmed, I'm sure," said the doctor. "I'm Doctor Skinner. Christopher and I share an interest."

Then he looked at his watch and raised an eyebrow.

"Is that the time! Well, it's been nice to meet you, Lauren … Christopher…" Doctor Skinner stared him right in the eye. "Until next time…"

And with that he was gone.

"What a creepy man," said Lauren with a shiver.

"You don't doe da half of dit…" muttered Christopher.

"What? Take that fake nose off. I can't hear a word you're saying."

Christopher pulled Little Big Nose away from his face and tucked him in his pocket.

"How do you know him?" asked Lauren.

"Erm … he's a fellow gardener," said Christopher. "We like to meet in the library occasionally and talk about … plants."

Lauren frowned at her brother. "I didn't know that."

"There are a lot of things about me you don't know."

"But why were you wearing that fake nose?"

Christopher face fell. "Erm…" He tried to think. "Well … I'm … I'm surprised you ask. Isn't it obvious?"

Lauren frowned even harder and then smiled.

"Oh yes. Silly me…"

"What?"

"But Halloween's not until next Saturday. Don't you think it's a bit early to be trying on your costume?"

Doctor Skinner paused at the front counter of the library. He turned to the severe woman behind the desk with his best smile.

"Before I go I just wanted to say how helpful a member of your staff has been."

98

"Oh thank you," said the woman with a tight little nod.

"Yes … the charming girl with the red hair and glasses. Now, what was her name? Lauren…"

"Lauren Postlethwaite." The woman took off her glasses and smiled for the first time that day, "She helps out at the weekend. She is the most delightful young lady."

"Isn't she just … Lauren *Postlethwaite*. Well, she's been very helpful … very helpful indeed."

Halloween Night

Mrs Postlethwaite watched the cloaked figure creep down the darkened hallway. A candle flickered through the blank eyes of a hollowed pumpkin, throwing dancing shadows of the hunched creature against the walls. Mrs Postlethwaite held her breath and edged open the kitchen door. Slowly the figure reached for the latch with trembling green fingers.

"Where do you think you're going?" demanded Mrs Postlethwaite and snapped on the hallway light.

Christopher spun round and sneezed loudly.

"Bless you."

"Danks," Christopher reached up to check that the large green nose was still stuck to his face, and then reluctantly met his mother's stare.

There it was again, *the look*.

"So?"

"Drick or Dreading…" said Christopher.

"With who?"

"The Edward dwins…"

"I happen to know for a fact that the Edwards are in the Isle Of White and besides, I can't remember the last time you played with the twins." Mrs Postlethwaite folded her arms. "Christopher, I do not like being lied to."

"I'll be absoludely fine!"

"I'm not having you wandering the streets on your own. If you really want to go, you can take your sister."

"Bud she's *younger* dan me…"

"I don't care … there's safety in numbers," Mrs Postlethwaite grabbed a sheet that was drying on a radiator and a pair of scissors from a kitchen drawer.

"Lauren!" She turned to Christopher. "You … wait there!" With that she disappeared up the stairs.

Christopher watched her go and then turned to the hallway mirror. With the cloak, the green face paint and the broomstick, he and Little Big Nose made a pretty good witch.

He reached up and patted the nose, "You all righd?"

"Fine," replied Little Big Nose. "You mother gave me quite a shock, that's all."

"Yeah, me doo…" said Christopher. "Id looks like Lauren's coming wid us, so you bedder keep quied."

"That's alright, I don't mind being quiet. It should be fun."

"Who you talking to?" Lauren pulled the sheet over her head and peered out through two makeshift holes.

"Do-one," said Christopher. "You call dat a cosdume?"

"Well, if you'd have told me you were going trick or treating I might have had more time to prepare…"

"Did id occur do you that I did nod dell you because I was happy enoud on my own."

"Well, aren't you the mysterious loner these days. Some day you're going to need friends, and…"

"Right, that's it you two!" Mrs Postlethwaite flew down the stairs and bundled them out of the door. "Stop arguing and off you go. Give me some peace and quiet for a change."

The front door slammed and Christopher and Lauren were alone together on the porch.

"Id's sdill a rubbish cosdume," said Christopher.

"Well, what are you supposed to be? The green goblin?"

"Look ad da broomsdick, sdupid."

"A zombie cleaning lady?"

"I'm obviously a widch, da cloak, da nose. Oh come on, leds ged going…"

"Slow down, I'm going to trip over my sheet…"

"I'm going do drip over my sheed! Ged a move on!"

Mrs Postlethwaite watched from the window as off they went, carrying an empty bucket, two terrors, squabbling into the night.

The evening was going well, so well in fact that they had to take turns to carry their bucket of sweets. Only one old man had refused to give them anything. Christopher had been keen to drop an egg through his letterbox, but Lauren argued against it.

"Most mean people are usually that way because they're sad and lonely, it doesn't seem right to make his life *more* miserable."

Christopher had reluctantly agreed not to trick the old man, but he secretly hoped that sooner or later they'd be able to trick *someone*.

All the while Little Big Nose silently clung to Christopher's face, thoroughly enjoying the whole experience. The damp fallen leaves gave off a wonderful rich aroma as Lauren and Christopher kicked them into the air, and each house had a different smell and a unique smiling face. Children shrieked with excitement in the distance and small goblins, trolls, monsters and vampires skipped along the streets and alleyways. He was learning that, like slugs, humans had their own special events and traditions … and he rather liked Halloween.

"This bucked's gedding really heavy," said

Christopher. "Led's just finish off this road den head back."

"Okey-dokey," said Lauren. She turned the corner to the next house's drive and stopped dead in her tracks. "Oh…"

"Whad is id? You seen a ghosd?"

Christopher chuckled at his joke.

Lauren reached up under her sheet and used it to wipe her glasses. She looked around her for a while.

"Whad's wrong wid you?"

"I … it's just …" Lauren looked to her brother and then back to the house. "Erm, its nothing … doesn't matter…" She shook her head.

"Righd shall we carry on den?"

"If you're sure you want to?"

"Course I'm sure, whad are you on aboud? Come on."

Christopher marched down to the door and rang the bell. He glanced back at his sister, who was still hesitating on the driveway. "Hurry up, we wand do ged the full effecd!"

Lauren scuttled up to her brother's side, "Listen Christopher, there's something I need to tell you … this house…"

"Well hello there, and what terrifying visions do I see before me?"

Christopher frowned. *That voice.*

He looked up to the man in the open doorway.

"Dad?"

104

The bucket slipped from his fingers. Little Big Nose sneezed in shock and slid right off his face.

Lauren raised her sheet and smiled awkwardly.

"Hiya, Dad."

Christopher reached down and quickly shoved Little Big Nose in his pocket. His father looked into the darkness.

"Chris? Is that you?" A huge smile spread across his face. "Great costume!" Suddenly he became very flustered.

"Do you need some more elastic for that nose? I think I've got some somewhere…"

Christopher turned and ran as fast as he could.

"Chris," said Mr Postlethwaite. "Don't go."

"Sorry Dad," said Lauren. "He didn't know it was your house. I should have told him. Here, take this." Lauren whipped off her sheet and ran after her brother.

By the time she caught up with him he was leaning against a lamp post, breathing in big gasps, tears rolling down his face.

"Christopher…"

He looked at her with blazing eyes. "Why didn't you tell me?"

"I'm sorry, I didn't plan it. I thought you might be happy."

Christopher ran his sleeve across his cheek, smudging his make-up.

"Happy, why would I be happy?" he shouted. "Don't you get it? I don't want to see him!"

"But Chris, you can't go through life without ever seeing him…"

"But that's what you don't understand!" A huge sob jolted his body but Christopher breathed it in and blinked back the tears. "I don't care if I *never* see him again," he said through gritted teeth.

"Christopher, you don't mean that."

"I do!" he yelled as he spun away. "Now leave me alone!"

"Christopher, I'm sorry! Wait for me … I'm sorry."

Christopher ran into the night and Lauren ran after him. Not so far away, their father quietly picked up the scattered sweets that littered his driveway and, with deliberate care, gently placed each one back into the discarded bucket.

Christopher gazed at the photo. The Christopher in the photo was obviously a lot younger, but his father was unchanged. They were both standing in an early version of Christopher's garden. The younger Christopher was almost hidden, smiling out from a tangled plant, a gardening fork in his hand. His father stood over him, leaning jauntily on a spade and looking off into the distance with a lopsided grin.

A sad wind moaned against the house and Christopher rested his elbows on the windowsill and looked out into the black night.

Little Big Nose rested on his shoulder.

"Is your father a bad man?" he whispered into his ear.

"Yes," said Christopher with a dark frown, and then uncertainly, "Well, sort of…"

He slumped forward and put his forehead against the windowpane. "Not really, I guess…"

"He never hurt you or was mean?"

"Well no, but that doesn't mean I have to like him."

"So what did he do that has upset you so much?"

Christopher took Little Big Nose from his shoulder and placed him down on the windowsill.

"What do you think he did?" he said. "He left…"

"But you can still see him whenever you want?"

"Yes."

"And he doesn't live far away…"

"No, but," Christopher got to his feet. "He still left didn't he?"

"But I don't see…"

"Everything was good before he went," said Christopher, his voice rising. "Everything was fine and then he had to leave and spoil it all. I hate him."

"I don't believe that to be true for a second."

Christopher collapsed back into his chair. "I don't want to talk about it."

The wind howled and a fox screeched somewhere in the night.

"You know," said Little Big Nose. "There's an old slug saying…"

"Here we go…" groaned Christopher.

"The old slug saying says that every trail starts with

love." Little Big Nose paused before adding, "Your father seemed very happy to see you today."

Christopher stomped over to his bed, "I said I don't want to talk about it!"

"You know I don't have a family anymore and I miss them very much…"

"Oh yeah?" said Christopher. "Well maybe you do. Maybe you do have a family. I mean, *Doctor Skinner made you!*"

"I don't think you can compare…"

"That makes him your dad, sort of, and you're not so eager to kiss and make up with him, are you?"

The moment he said it, Christopher regretted it.

There was a stony silence.

"I think," said the nose, "that I should rather like to go for a trundle around the garden."

"Little Big Nose…"

"Please."

Christopher sighed and walked over to the nose. He picked up his friend, opened the window and placed him on the branch that the nose used to get to and from the garden.

"Erm … Little Big Nose, I'm sorry. I didn't mean it."

"I know," said the nose. "I just think that both of us could use a good think."

"I'm sorry." Christopher watched his friend crawl along the branch down to the garden. "Goodnight…" Little Big Nose sniffed the air once or twice and then disappeared into a bush.

Christopher shut the window and drew the curtains. He looked at the picture of his dad one last time and then sloped off to bed. Before he turned off the light he placed the photo back under his pillow.

The Monster in
the Garden

An icy wind chased around the Postlethwaite garden, shaking the leaves and bending the trees. Rain whipped against the ground and thunder rolled around the

clouds. All the creatures of the garden hid silently in their nests and holes.

There was one figure, sitting on top of a rock in Christopher's patch of land, who seemed oblivious to the weather…

Arnold the gnome proudly held his rod aloft, smiled firmly and sat in silence as the storm spun around him. He'd seen worse.

Suddenly a bush began to shake with the sound of twigs snapping and angry muttering. A large foot appeared and crunched down upon the gnome. Arnold shattered into tiny jagged pieces.

"I can't see a blasted thing," grumbled Doctor Skinner as he stepped out of the bush. "What is all this junk?"

The doctor clattered through Christopher's displays, knocking over soldiers and zombie dolls, stepping in swamps and tripping over caves.

"Get out of the way … what a load of old tat … oops…" With a lurch and a stumble the doctor was free of the jumbled chaos.

He brushed himself down and looked through the row of little trees to the house.

"The only Postlethwaites in the town." He chuckled. "This must be the place."

Doctor Skinner reached into his pocket and pulled out a limp Scuttler.

"Well, my little five-fingered friend, this could be your finest hour." He placed the hand on the ground. "Let's get this show on the road."

From his other pocket, Doctor Skinner produced Scuttler's remote control, held together by tape.

"Got to stop stamping on things when they don't work…" He pressed a knob and the controls whirred to life.

Scuttler twitched. The eye opened slowly and stared at the doctor.

The tiny monitor crackled and Doctor Skinner inspected it.

"Have to engage night vision, I think." He flicked a switch, Scuttler's eyeball glowed a dark red and the monitor revealed a hands-eye view of the garden.

"Brilliant. All systems go."

The doctor furrowed his brow and pushed a big red button. The hand rose to its fingertips and tensed, like a sprinter waiting for the starting pistol.

"On your marks, get set … GO!" The Doctor furiously fiddled with the remote and Scuttler was off, scampering across the grass. Its fingers were a blur of motion as it wove through the garden toward the house. The hand stopped by the back door and the glowing red eye stared upwards at an opened window.

"Excellent," said Doctor Skinner. "But how to get up there?"

He twiddled a lever and the eyeball scanned around. A drainpipe came into view.

Doctor Skinner pawed the control sticks and began to sing quietly to himself.

"Incy wincy spider ... crawling up the spout..." Scuttler grabbed the drainpipe and began to grapple up the side of the house. "Creep inside the bedroom and take the nosey out."

The hand leapt from the drainpipe to the windowsill with quiet expertise.

"Almost there. Here we go ... oopsy daisy."

Scuttler eased through the window and landed on the bedroom floor with a quiet thud.

Doctor Skinner looked at the monitor. "Now ... where are we?"

A teddy bear lay abandoned on the floor.

"Well ... it's definitely a kid's room. Let's see whose!"

Scuttler crawled over the bear and toward the bed.

Doctor Skinner's tongue poked out of the corner of his mouth with concentration. "Must be extra quiet."

Scuttler slowly bent its knuckles and then pounced upon the bed sheet.

The red eyeball swivelled, throwing a dark orange glow upon Lauren's sleeping face.

"Rats. Wrong brat. But the boy can't be far away."

Scuttler crept to the edge of the bed and hopped to the floor ... then the screen went blank.

"What?" The doctor shook the remote and banged it with his fist.

Nothing.

His cheeks flushed deep purple as the rain whipped around him.

He closed his eyes tight and whispered to himself.

113

"Calm down … calm down. It's probably just out of range."

As he crept through the row of trees he sucked deep breaths through his clenched teeth. "Get a little closer and try again…"

He got as near to the house as he dared. "Let's hope no-one's up…"

The porch lights picked out his shining eyes as he stood silhouetted against the shaking trees. "Okay, you'd better work now or there's going to be big trouble."

He looked down to the dead controls, and noticed a small movement out of the corner of his eye and heard a familiar snuffle.

"What have we here?"

He peered down into the darkness, and a dreadful grin spread across his face.

The bad weather had caught Little Big Nose by surprise during his midnight trundle, so he had decided to get under the bush and sit it out.

"Just the specimen I'm looking for!"

Doctor Skinner's six fingers grabbed him. Little Big Nose opened his nostrils and screamed for help.

But no one heard.

His slug distress call was soon lost in the night, drowned by the rain … swallowed up by the storm.

Screams in
the Morning

That morning Christopher was woken up by a high-pitched scream. Lauren burst though the door in her nightie, jumped on to the end of his bed and hugged her knees tight to her chest.

Christopher glared over the edge of his duvet. "Get out. I'm not talking to you."

"I'm really sorry about last night."

"No you're not."

"I am, truly. I didn't have time to think." She shivered. "Anyway. I don't care if you're still angry with me, I'm not leaving this bed until you've got rid of it."

"Got rid of what?"

"The thing in my room."

"Oh no … not again."

"But, this ones … this one's huge!"

"It's just a tiny harmless creature…"

"I promise to you that this is the biggest spider I have seen in my entire life!"

Christopher sat up on his elbows and glowered at his sister. She was staring at his door intently, as if she expected a monster to burst into the room at any moment.

"You're not even wearing your glasses!" he cried, falling back into bed. "It's probably nothing, like the time you thought that scarf was a snake."

"That was years ago," said Lauren. "And besides, when a spider that gigantic is in your room, you don't stop to put your glasses on!"

"Why is it always me who has to deal with these emergencies? What's wrong with Mum?"

Lauren stuck out her bottom lip. "I don't know … you're just better with stuff like this. You're good with animals. I know you won't hurt it."

"So even though you think it's the biggest most dangerous looking spider you have ever seen…"

"Possibly an African species. They sometimes get shipped over in banana boxes…"

"…you don't want me to hurt it."

Lauren jumped from the bed and pulled at Christopher's arm.

"Come on, please Christopher. I promise this is the last time…"

Christopher grumpily lurched from the bed. "It better be, he said.

Lauren took his hand and led him out to the landing.

"It's all right … I'm coming," Christopher shook his hand free. "What have I told you about grabbing my hand?"

"Everything alright up there?" yelled Mrs Postlethwaite.

"Fine, Mum," replied Christopher. "Just another infestation of man-eating super spiders in Lauren's room."

"You wait to *you* see it," muttered Lauren. "You won't be laughing then."

Christopher grabbed a pen and edged closer. Scuttler was lying palm upwards on the floor, like a dead crab. Christopher knelt down as close as he dared to the lifeless hand.

Lauren stood in the corner of the room biting her fingernails. "Throw it out the window…"

"Be quiet…"

The pen trembled as Christopher reached across and poked.

The fingers twitched and Christopher jumped backwards with a yelp.

"It's not so funny now, is it?" said Lauren. "Is it dead?"

Christopher pulled himself together and took another look. Scuttler hadn't moved. "I'm not sure…" He glanced at the electronic device on Scuttler's wrist. It didn't seem to be active. None of the lights were flashing. He was pretty sure the machine wasn't on.

Christopher breathed in and braced himself. He squeezed his eyes shut and quickly grabbed one of Scuttler's fingers. The hand flinched a little and then was still.

Lauren put on her glasses and crept across the room.

"What do you think it is?" She looked over her brother's shoulder. "I told you it was too big to come from…"

The words stuck in her throat as her eyes focussed on Scuttler.

Christopher turned around to face his trembling sister.

"What … what is that?"

"It's okay," he said. "I think its batteries must have run out or something…"

"Batteries? What do you mean, batteries?"

Christopher stood up and placed his hands on Lauren's shoulders.

"Listen, I know what it is…" Christopher looked into his sister's eyes. "But if I tell you, you have to promise to keep him a secret."

"Keep who a secret?"

"Little Big Nose."

Christopher froze.

"Oh no … Little Big Nose!" he shouted and ran from the room.

"Little Big what?" Lauren glanced down at the hand. "Christopher, don't just leave me here with this thing … Christopher, WAIT!"

Nosenapped

"He's gone," said Christopher as he threw the empty shoebox to the floor. "Nosenapped."

"Who's gone?"

"Doctor Skinner's nosenapped him."

Lauren frowned angrily at her brother. "Christopher, I am *this* close to calling Mum and telling her there is a dead hand in my bedroom."

"No wait … don't…" Christopher flopped onto his bed. "I'll tell you … I'll tell you everything."

And so Lauren learned the secret of the nose. Christopher started at the beginning and told the entire story. He told Lauren about finding Little Big Nose stuck to Arnold's face, he told her about all the slug sayings and riddles and about Doctor Skinner's mansion.

"In fact, you met the doctor and Little Big Nose at the library!"

"I remember Doctor Skinner, but I don't remember any nose…"

"He was stuck to my face. He came out with us on Halloween as well."

Lauren sat on the bed and sighed. "Christopher, I'm finding all of this very hard to believe … it just sounds so … so crazy."

"I knew it," said Christopher. "You think it's just me being odd, you think I'm making this up."

"I didn't say that."

Christopher got up and stalked from the room, banging the door. Seconds later the door flew open and Christopher appeared brandishing the lifeless Scuttler. He held it up in front of Lauren's face.

"Christopher, please don't, it's horrible…"

"If all this is in my imagination," said Christopher, waving the hand in front of her. "Then how do you explain this?"

"Okay … okay, I believe you. Just please put it down. CHRISTOPHER!"

Christopher dropped Scuttler to the floor and stared out of the window.

"I've got to help Little Big Nose," he said quietly. "Doctor Skinner's going to cut him up into tiny bits, I know he is…"

"But Christopher what can you do?"

"I'm going to have to go over there, tonight, after bedtime." He looked Lauren in the eye. "And you're going to cover for me. If Mum finds out I'm not here, just tell her I've gone camping or something…"

"Christopher…"

"You're smart, you'll think of something."

"But it could be dangerous and it's going to be dark," pleaded Lauren.

"It's a full moon tonight, that should give me enough light to find my way around."

"I don't think you should go…" Lauren got slowly from the bed and walked over to her brother. "Maybe we should tell Mum."

"She won't believe us. And even if she did, what could she do?"

A single tear fell down Lauren's cheek.

"Oh Lauren…" Christopher gave his sister's arm an awkward little rub. "I'll be fine, I promise. It's just … I've got to do something. Little Big Nose is my friend, and if you're not there for your friends when they need you, then you're not any kind of friend at all."

"I know. But there must be another way…"

"No," said Christopher firmly. "If I don't do

something soon, then Little Big Nose is in big trouble."

He looked toward the black clouds that smothered the sky. Tiny shards of icy snow swirled down from the darkness. "There's nothing else for it. I've got to go to Skinner's mansion."

WINTER

WINTER

The Trail Through the Snow

Christopher looked up at the wall and shivered. Things were not going well.

When he left the house he had been far too eager to

get going, and he hadn't thought twice about the layer of snow on the ground or the chill in the air. After ten minutes on the road, his bike had skidded on some ice. He grazed his knee, and his hands had been far too cold to fix the disconnected gears. He hid his bike in a nearby hedge, and had to walk the rest of the way, only to find Doctor Skinner's gates locked. He trudged halfway round the doctor's land, but he couldn't see any way under or over the tall wall that protected it. His shoes were soaking, his hands were red raw and every inch of him was cold.

He stumbled to a halt and watched heavy black clouds sweep overhead, blotting out the stars and the full moon.

"Typical me…" he mumbled.

He'd blundered into his rescue mission full of friendship and bravery, but didn't have any plans of how to get into the mansion and save his friend.

He stared into the blackness of the night and felt utterly alone.

Two green eyes stared back.

Christopher's whole body stiffened.

A damp muzzle sniffed the air and a paw rose tentatively from the ground.

Christopher stood as still as possible.

The paw sunk into a crust of snow and a thick auburn tail swished restlessly from side to side.

For a moment Christopher forgot where he was and the terrible cold, and was once again just a boy, a boy who adored animals.

The fox surveyed him with shining eyes. She was obviously old, with a few scars and greying fur, but the sight of her, stark and brilliant against the snow, took Christopher's breath away.

They looked at each other.

Her ears twitched, and Christopher was sure she could hear his heart pounding.

She made the first move. Never once taking her eyes from the boy, the fox dipped her head and sniffed the snow.

Christopher's thoughts returned to the matter in hand. If only he could talk to her, like Little Big Nose, and explain … she could help.

He took a furtive step toward her.

"Hello there…" Before he could say any more, the fox flinched backwards and hastily loped away.

Christopher's shoulders slumped.

"Stupid idea anyway," he said. "Can't say I blame you either. What have humans ever done for foxes?"

He crouched down in the snow and put his head in his hands.

He looked mournfully at the fox's tracks and wished he could ask Little Big Nose what to do.

Then he frowned.

Then he smiled.

The fox's tracks headed away from him … but they also headed towards Doctor Skinner's perimeter wall.

Christopher jumped to his feet.

"She might help me yet…"

He set off, hot on the fox's trail.

Eyeballs, feet, toes, teeth, elbows, ears, belly buttons and knees spun past over and over again, their shapes and smells distorted, thundering by with sickening speed. Like a sprawling lifeless creature, each specimen blurred into the next, pale hands reached out to nothing and countless mouths opened to empty screams.

Little Big Nose could no longer tell one smell from the next. As he spun round and round, the different odours of the laboratory flashed by so quickly that he felt dizzy and ill.

"Had enough yet?" Doctor Skinner turned up the speed on the centrifuge and giggled. "Scream if you want to go faster!"

Little Big Nose was strapped, nostrils outwards, to the middle of the machine. Like a high-speed roundabout, the centrifuge spun at such an incredibly fast rate that if he hadn't been fastened down, the nose would have been thrown off long ago. As it was, the force of the spinning machine sucked all the snot from his nostrils, which ran into the beakers and test tubes that were attached to the edge of the device. He felt as if his life was being slowly drained away.

Doctor Skinner reached down and flicked a switch.

"I think you've had enough for now." The centrifuge slowly wound down to a halt.

The Doctor unhooked a beaker filled with dark green snot and held it up to the light.

"This should be interesting."

Little Big Nose wheezed desperately. With what

was left of his strength he opened his nostril and cried out a slug distress call.

"What's that infernal racket you keep making?" asked Doctor Skinner as he raised a thick magnifying glass to his eye.

"A message for my friends," said the nose.

"Ah … friends…" chuckled the doctor. "Never really had much call for them. Don't have time you see, too busy being a genius."

"Even a genius needs friends…"

"Not me," said Skinner as he inspected the mucus.

Little Big Nose felt so empty and drained that he just wanted to sleep. He knew instinctively, however, that it was a bad idea. He must keep talking, it would keep him awake and it might buy him some time.

"What do you want?" he asked weakly.

"Well," replied the doctor, ever eager to follow up a question about his work. "I want to know why you're alive."

"I'm alive because my mother and Christopher both saved me when I was alone and helpless."

"That's very charming," replied the doctor. "But my research will be of a more scientific nature."

Skinner pulled out a microscope and placed the beaker of goo underneath the long lens.

"A long time ago, my father taught me a valuable lesson," continued the doctor as he fiddled with the focus. "He taught it to me over and over again as it happens, but it was a lesson worth learning and I am eternally grateful to him."

"And where is your father now?" asked Little Big Nose.

Doctor Skinner ignored the question.

"My father taught me that all living things, even us humans are no more or less than very well-made machines. And one day we will understand everything there is to know about animals and humans, by using science and science alone."

"I hope that isn't so…" said the nose. "I'd like to think life has a little more magic to it than that."

"It doesn't, I'm afraid," said Skinner. "No … we're all machines, whether you like it or not."

The doctor paused thoughtfully. "And it is this realisation that has been the inspiration for all my devices. If humans and technology are basically machines then why not mix the two?"

"But the part of the me that is alive," said Little Big Nose. "The part of me that hopes and feels … that isn't a machine."

The doctor snorted.

The nose continued, "And you won't discover what it is by examining a test tube of mucus."

"You'd better hope I can," said the doctor in a cold voice. He reached into a drawer and pulled out a long shining scalpel. "Because if I can't … I will have to cut you open to find out."

The tracks led to a corner of the wall where a few bricks had fallen away. Beneath these bricks was a dirt path dug into the earth and worn smooth by years of use by generations of foxes.

Christopher took the rucksack off his back and thrust it through the hole. After a moment or two of kicking the snow away from the entrance to the tunnel, he got onto his hands and knees and began to scramble through.

There was more snow built up on the other side of the wall, so Christopher had to thrust it away with his freezing hands. He grabbed the roots of a nearby tree and pulled.

Nothing.

He tugged again, but didn't move an inch. He tried to wriggle out the way he had come but found he couldn't move backwards either. He was stuck tight.

"This isn't good."

He attempted to dig his elbows into the ground, but it was hard and icy. He held his breath and heaved.

Panic crept up his neck and itched into his mouth.

In a mad burst of energy he thrashed about in the snow, kicking his feet and beating the wall with his fists. He gritted his teeth and pushed against the stone as hard as he could, hot steam rising from his face.

Still nothing.

"Help!" The cry rose to his throat before he had time to control it. It echoed amongst the leafless trees and then faded into the night.

An owl watched him with cold eyes. It blinked, shook its feathers and then took to the air, swooping silently away.

Numbness was beginning to spread through his toes and fingers. If he didn't get out soon he was going to freeze to death.

"Help!" he yelled at the top of his voice. "Help … somebody … anybody … please … help!"

"Shhh, be quiet," a harsh whispered voice came from the other side of the wall.

Christopher felt a pair of small hands grab him by the ankles.

"Just relax and I'll try my best to push you through."

Before Christopher could say anything the hands started pushing and he was moving. He grabbed at the tree trunk, pulled himself clear and flopped on to the snow, panting heavily.

A woolly hat edged by ginger hair appeared at the hole. Lauren looked up at her brother with red cheeks and sparkling eyes.

"I knew you'd need my help sooner or later." She held out a gloved hand. "Don't just sit there, give me a pull."

Christopher reached down and heaved his sister through the hole and on to her feet.

"What are you doing here?"

"I followed you."

"I told you to stay at home!"

"I was worried," said Lauren.

"I don't care if you were worried, this could be dangerous!"

"You would have been stuck there all night!"

"I wouldn't have … I had it all under control … I was going to…" Christopher tailed off and then looked down at his hand with a huge scowl on his face.

Lauren followed his gaze.

"Oh right … sorry". She hadn't even noticed that she was still holding his hand. She let go and hung her head.

"I just do it by accident some times … I don't…" she began to try to explain but then stopped when she noticed her brother's hands. "LOOK AT YOUR FINGERS! They're red raw!"

Christopher tucked them under his armpits, "I'm all right."

"Didn't you bring any gloves?" Looking at Lauren in her mittens, hat, wellies and scarf, Christopher did feel a bit underprepared … and very cold.

"Isn't there anything in your rucksack?" she asked. "What did you bring?"

Christopher paused and then muttered something.

"What?" said Lauren.

"MY SPY KIT, OKAY?" shouted Christopher.

"Spy kit?" Lauren couldn't suppress her giggle. "What for?"

"It's got all sorts of useful stuff!" Christopher delved into his bag. "Look, erm … binoculars … invisible ink pen…"

"Very useful."

"A compass. I don't think that works anymore but…"

"No gloves though."

"Walkie-talkies!" said Christopher triumphantly, holding up one of the set. "Little radios so we can talk to each other. Very handy seeing as Mum won't let us have phones till we're older. You never know when you might need these!"

"But you didn't bring any gloves…"

"No…"

"Or any food."

"I'm not hungry."

"That's a shame." Lauren reached down through the hole in the wall and pulled out a rucksack of her own. "Because I brought along some chocolate." As soon as she'd taken the bar from the front pouch Christopher snatched it, ripped off the wrapper and devoured the whole thing in two mouthfuls.

"Now something for those hands, give me that…" Lauren took the walkie-talkie from Christopher and handed him two bright pink gloves.

"I'm not wearing these," said Christopher but put the gloves on away. Lauren wrapped a scarf around his neck and put a bobble hat on his head.

"That's better," she said, standing back to survey her work.

"Whoever embarked on a daring rescue mission looking like this?" said Christopher as he turned and strode out across the snow. "And another thing," he called over his shoulder. "If anything bad happens to you, remember whose idea it was to follow me."

As they walked on, a host of eyelids opened high

above them. In the uppermost reaches of Doctor Skinner's wood, amongst the tallest branches, perched a hoard of darkly glistening spheres. As the children weaved through the trees a hundred red pupils followed them with lifeless precision. Then the eyeballs began to gently buzz as, one by one, their antennas slowly rose into the air.

"What am I missing?" The doctor sent the microscope clattering to the floor. "I was sure your mucus would hold the answer."

"Maybe you're looking in the wrong places," said Little Big Nose.

"You know what?" replied Skinner. "I think I'm going to enjoy dissecting you."

"INTRUDERS! INTRUDERS!" A mouth that was mounted on to a wall began shouting loudly. "WARNING! INTRUDERS!"

Monitors crackled, and Little Big Nose snorted with joy when Christopher and Lauren walked into shot.

The doctor stalked over to his security terminal. "How did they get in?"

"I knew my friends would come," said the nose.

"They won't be here long though," growled the doctor. "I can assure you of that!"

He furiously grabbed at levers and flicked switches.

"I have a device designed specifically for trespassers. And your friends are not going to like it!"

The Mechanical Beast

"Wait!"

Christopher threw his arms into the air. "What is it now?"

Lauren stood a few yards behind him with a look of concentration on her face.

EEEK!

"Come on!" said Christopher. "We haven't got time to be resting every few minutes."

"Will you just be quiet!" The sharpness in her voice stopped him dead. "Can you hear that?"

Christopher listened. The wind moaned through the trees, but there was nothing else.

"I can't hear anything," he said. "You're just imaginings things … can we get going now, please?"

Lauren reached down, cleared a patch in the snow and held her hand flat against the ground.

"What are you doing?"

"Sshhh!"

The winter soil throbbed against her fingers.

She pushed down harder. A drum roll of muffled thuds rumbled through the earth.

"Something's coming," she said. With every second the thuds became more insistent. "And whatever it is … it's coming fast."

They heard a splintered crack as a distant tree crashed to the ground.

Lauren jumped unsteadily to her feet, "Now do you believe me?"

Suddenly the ground was shaking beneath them. The heavy thuds surrounded them, echoing around the trees.

The whole wood began to tremble. Snow fell from branches and a murder of crows lurched screeching into sky.

Panic pumped through Christopher's veins. He span around wildly, searching the gloom.

Then, trunk and bark split and snapped as trees were ripped from their roots and cast aside like matchsticks.

Legs and arms burst through the destruction and skidded to a halt.

Lauren and Christopher stood frozen, stiff with fear. Countless beady eyes blinked and stared about wildly. Then one by one their pupils shrank to pinpricks as they focused on the children.

With a low mechanical growl two large metal plates slid aside to reveal row upon row of sharpened human teeth.

Christopher turned to Lauren.

"Run!"

The snow was thick and slippery beneath them and branches and twigs scraped across their faces and snagged their clothes. Christopher's heartbeat thudded in his throat.

"Don't look back!"

They blundered blindly through the wood, sprawling this way and that, pushing through hedges and trees. Christopher risked a glance over his shoulder.

The huge creature, half flesh half machine, thundered after them. Like a boulder crashing down a mountain it tumbled over and over on its many arms and legs, destroying anything in its path. With each roll it gathered speed and drew closer, filling the air with the creaks and snaps of shattering wood.

"Christopher!" Lauren turned to her brother and blinked through her steamed up glasses. "I can't see!"

Christopher grabbed her arm.

"Just keep going! Watch out for…" Too late. Lauren's foot hit a large twisted root and she slid, face down, through the snow. Christopher rushed to her side and yanked her to her feet.

"Christopher, I tripped…" Lauren stumbled in a daze. Icy snow covered her face except for a large graze that ran across her forehead.

"Let's get you clean," Christopher hastily brushed the snow from her cheeks.

Then he froze.

Hot wet breath panted against the back of his neck.

Lauren looked blankly from behind her misted glasses.

"Chris … what's going on?"

"Just don't move," he whispered. A deep mechanical growl cut through the air and a thick moist cloud of breath enveloped his head.

Christopher turned around … very slowly.

The growl continued, grating along like the low thrum of a chainsaw.

"What's going on, Chris?" Lauren was wiping frantically at her lenses.

Christopher faced row upon row of needle sharp teeth. He edged back, putting himself between Lauren and the creature.

The mechanised beast pulled itself up to full height. Fingers, arms and toes twitched.

Lauren peered over her brother's shoulder. She

opened her mouth to scream but found she had no breath.

"Stay calm," said Christopher, reaching down for a rock.

The huge metal ball towered above them, held aloft by arms and legs that padded heavily from side to side. Countless limbs protruded from the machine at every angle. Some held it upright, others clutched the surrounding trees whilst others swayed through the air. Beyond the limbs, encrusted on the iron sphere like barnacles, a thousand eyes blinked and watched the children. At the centre, the huge mouth, its metal plated lips pulled back and panted heavily. Three long wet tongues slithered around the teeth like snakes. The machine growled again, louder this time. The growl grew in volume and venom, gathering force like an airplane engine, building to an ear-shattering roar.

Christopher shouted over the creature's din. "Lauren ... when I say, I want you to run!"

He pulled his arm back and tightened his grip on the rock.

"Have you got that?"

"Christopher ... I'm not leaving."

"Just get ready to run..." Christopher took aim. "Don't argue. When I say..."

Lauren saw a flash of flesh and heard a sickening thud as her brother was swatted from her side like an insect. Christopher flew through the air and slammed against a tree trunk. Lauren watched in horror as his limp body slid to the floor.

Then her world spun upside down as two fat fists whisked her from the ground. There was a blur of trees and clouds as the arms lifted her higher. Then all she could see were teeth, row upon row of yellow sharpened fangs. Lauren looked down at the gaping maw and screamed. The tongues squirmed and thrashed and the metal plated lips retracted further. The waiting mouth grew wide and hungry.

"This is all such incredible fun!" shouted Skinner. Before him, a thousand tiny monitors transmitted images from the creature's beady eyes. Lauren dangled and silently screamed from countless different angles.

"I think she's just about scared enough don't you?" said the Doctor pointing to a close-up of Lauren's terrified face.

"Don't hurt her…" said Little Big Nose.

"I'm not going to hurt her!" blustered the Doctor. "I'm just going to dump her and her brother over the wall. I don't think they'll be coming back, do you?"

Skinner jiggled a joystick that lowered Lauren even closer to the gaping mouth.

"I can't guarantee that she won't have nightmares for the rest of her life though!"

The doctor winked at the nose and then tuned his attention back to his computer terminal. He pushed the lever again and then frowned.

"What the…?" the doctor jabbed at buttons and glared at monitors. Lauren remained dangling in mid air. "Nothing's responding…"

Gradually, the mechanical hum that had filled the room fell silent as every computer display died.

The doctor pushed frantically at his controls and watched helplessly as the fists that clenched Lauren lost their grip. The girl dropped deep into the creature's mouth and the metal jaws clenched shut. Then all other power to the mechanical beast faded, and its legs and arms gave way. The thousand tiny monitors showed the ground lurch and rise to greet the dying beast and then each and every screen buzzed to black.

Tears Turn to Ice

Christopher traced the edges of the metal plating with his fingers.

"There has to be some way in…" he muttered.

The ball was impenetrable.

After it had shuddered to the ground, every limb retreated into the machine and two thick iron plates had slid sharply over the mouth.

Only the eyes remained, lifeless and blank, staring into nothing. Christopher felt around one of the eyeballs for a sign of weakness, but it was useless. Each one was welded into place. There was no way in … or out of the ball.

Christopher felt all strength, all hope seep from his heart. He slumped back into the snow and looked at the machine.

His sister was in there.

He didn't even know if she had survived the teeth.

In a way he hoped not. He couldn't bear to think of her trapped in its belly, screaming as the air ran out.

He hung his head and wept.

He thought of all the times she had tried to take his hand. Now all he wanted to do was hold hers.

But it was too late.

Lauren was gone.

"I don't understand it!" The doctor ripped away the panels to his main computer system. "What could have caused so much damage?"

He peered into the terminal and got his answer.

"Where did you all come from?"

There were hundreds of them, munching away at the wires and circuitry that made his computerised kingdom work.

"I've heard of computer bugs…" he said. "But computer slugs?"

Christopher sat in a world of his own and watched his tears slowly turn to ice.

It took a while for the small voice to pierce his dark contemplation.

"Christopher ... Christopher..."

The voice was muffled. Christopher jumped to his feet and looked frantically around. "Where's it coming from?"

"Christopher ... can you hear me? Over and out..."

His walkie-talkie. Christopher scrabbled in his pockets.

He held the handset up to his mouth.

"Lauren! Is that you? Are you all right?"

"Just about..." came the weak reply. "But I don't want to be in here much longer I've found a panel with a handle on it ... but it won't open ... it's jammed. Can you hear that?"

Christopher rushed to the ball and could just make out a faint knocking, coming from beneath the machine.

"It must be wedged against the ground," said Christopher. "Hang on..."

Christopher searched the nearby trees and returned with a rock and large branch. Wedging the rock by the ball, he thrust in the branch over it and under the machine to make a lever.

"Hang on!" he shouted. Christopher thrust all his weight down on to the branch. With a deep creak the ball rolled a metre or two and then stopped.

A panel banged open and a small pink hand thrust into the air.

Christopher grabbed his sister's hand and pulled her free.

"Are you okay? You're not hurt are you?" he said as he hugged her close.

"I'm fine…" said Lauren shyly. "Don't fuss."

"Rubbish!" said Christopher and planted a big wet sloppy kiss on her forehead. "I'll make a fuss of you if I want!"

Lauren beamed and handed him back his walkie-talkie.

"I told you my spy kit would come in handy," said Christopher.

"You'll need more than a kids' spy kit to help you now…"

The children turned and gasped. Doctor Skinner emerged from behind a tree.

"You two," he said, "have been the most dreadful nuisance."

They spun on their heels, but the Doctor's long limbs were too quick. His bony fingers grabbed their coats and hoisted them into the air.

The Doctor eyed the pair with a terrible twinkle in his eye. "What am I going to do with you?"

The Laboratory

"Christopher, I'm scared."

Christopher squeezed his sister's hand.

"Me too." He tried his best to smile. "But it'll be okay. I'll think of something."

"Oh no," said Lauren trying to smile back at him. "We're in worse trouble than I thought."

Christopher had to admit that their situation wasn't good. They were locked in a small cage, in the laboratory

of a madman who was just about to cut Little Big Nose into tiny pieces. Things couldn't get much worse.

"Sitting comfortably, are we?" Doctor Skinner leant over and rattled his scalpel along the bars.

"Not really!" said Christopher. The cage was barely big enough for him and his sister. They had to crouch awkwardly and crane their necks to fit.

"Well, it is designed for monkeys after all," said the doctor as he rose to his full height. "I don't have any cages specifically for children. But with the amount of bother you and your friends have caused me today, I might have to build one."

Doctor Skinner held up a large jar filled with slugs. "Who would have guessed that such small, slimy, horrible pests could wreak such havoc ... and these shell-less molluscs haven't helped much either!"

He exploded into a fit of giggles and spun off across the laboratory.

The slugs had indeed wreaked havoc. Most of the doctor's machines and computers were not working and even the lights were down. Candles flickered around the room, illuminating the lifeless specimens. Above all this, the low clouds smothered the turret in a thick black mist. There was nothing to be seen beyond the glass dome roof: no sky, no stars, no moon. Just an immense swirling darkness.

Lauren and Christopher huddled closer together.

"I'll get us out of here," whispered Christopher. "I promise."

"And how is the patient feeling?" asked Skinner as he reeled over to Little Big Nose. The nose was once again strapped down, this time to a table in the middle of the room. Surrounding him were various metal implements, clamps, knives and scalpels of all sizes. The doctor stood above him and pulled on a rubber glove.

"Six fingered," he said and winked. "I have them specially made."

"Please, doctor..." said Little Big Nose. "Please think about what you're doing."

"I am thinking about it, you insufferable snout," replied the doctor. "This dissection must go ahead ... for the sake of science."

"What about me?"

Doctor Skinner paused and stared hard at the nose. "I do wish you'd shut up. Here I am on the verge of a great discovery. Possibly the most important day of my life and you're spoiling the whole mood."

"You can choose," whispered the nose. "Choose to be kind."

Doctor Skinner shook his head. "No, no, no. When it comes to an important scientific discovery like this, there is no choice. As my father used to say – you can't make an omelette without cracking a few eggs!"

"And where is your father now?"

Christopher looked round the room in hope of inspiration.

"Haven't you got any bar cutters or skeleton keys in your spy kit?" asked Lauren.

Christopher didn't answer. He felt scared and lost and angry and resolute all at the same time. The worse thing was that he'd got Lauren into this. He couldn't let anything happen to her. He'd already nearly lost her once and was determined not to let that happen again. He had to think.

His eyes fell on the overloaded bin that sat in the nearest corner of the room.

"Look at that," whispered Christopher and pointed.

"What?" she said "Just a load of old rubbish."

"No look, right on the very top…"

Lauren pushed up her glasses and squinted.

"Looks like some kind of remote control."

"Exactly," said Christopher and delved into his bag. "And what's written on it?"

"Erm, hang on, its difficult to read. Let me see." Lauren scrunched up her eyes. "It says S something … Scuffler … no hang on…"

"Quiet over there!" shouted Doctor Skinner over his shoulder. "I need silence!"

"I did bring something else I thought might be useful," whispered Christopher. He held open his bag a fraction so Lauren could see inside. "I didn't mention it because I know it gives you the willies."

Lauren peered into Christopher's rucksack and a huge smile spread across her face.

"Why are you so fascinated by my father?"

"Because I want to know more about you."

The Doctor surveyed the table and his various implements, then glanced at the nose. "For pity's sake ... why?"

"Because you created me," said Little Big Nose. "I may not like it ... but you are where my trail begins."

"And where it ends," replied the doctor in a cold, hard voice.

"I don't believe that..."

"Believe it, snout! I'm afraid you are a necessary sacrifice in the name of progress."

"Would your father be proud?"

Doctor Skinner closed his eyes and said, as calmly as he could, "My father is of little importance any more."

"Why?"

"None of your business!"

"Is he still alive?"

"I don't know!"

The nose was perplexed. "You don't know if your father is alive or dead? That's odd."

"Not odd at all, you nosey ... you nosey nose!"

"Well, it seems odd to me."

"Not to me," growled the Doctor.

"Why?"

"Because he LEFT! He left and never came back." The doctor raised his fists and paced around the table. "He left when I was a child, and I haven't seen or heard from him since. There, now you know! Does that satisfy your infuriating curiosity?"

"You must be angry with him," said the nose quietly.

"He was an amazing scientist ... a very intelligent, brilliant man."

"But not a good father."

"Will you shut up?" said the doctor. "How am I supposed to operate when you keep asking stupid infantile questions?"

"If the questions are stupid ... why are you so upset?"

The doctor glared at the nose with bulging eyes.

"Upset?" A big blue vein pulsed in his forehead and his fists were clenched tight. "I ... AM ... NOT ... UPSET!"

Little Big Nose could almost smell the anger as the Doctor stood there, stiff with rage.

Then ... Doctor Skinner laughed.

"How could a tiny little thing like you upset me on a day like today." He spread his long arms out. "On this glorious day of discovery... in fact..." Skinner clicked his fingers. "I should be filming this! The only witnesses I have are two dimwit children and a snotty hooter. No, this won't do..."

Doctor Skinner clapped his hands together and swept out of the laboratory. Christopher and Lauren watched him go. This was their chance.

"It's no use." Christopher was at full stretch. His face was pushed against the cage bars but his fingers were still inches short of the bin. He turned to Lauren and whispered. "I can't reach."

"Christopher?" It was Little Big Nose, calling weakly from the table.

"It's okay!" shouted Christopher. "Keep him talking, we've got a plan." He turned to his sister and said in a low voice, "Just listen to him, he's not well, I'm not sure how long he's going to last."

Lauren frowned and thought as hard as she could. She was annoyed with herself. She was supposed to be the clever one but so far she'd been useless. She'd made fun of Christopher and his spy kit, but it had already been more helpful than anything she'd brought. All she'd packed was some chocolate and winter clothes.

The thought hit her so suddenly that she jumped and banged her head on the cage, "Got it! Ow!"

"Watch out," said Christopher. "Got what?"

"Come here…" Lauren reached over to her brother and unwound the scarf from around his neck. She then grabbed her scarf and tied them together.

"You should be able to reach it with this," she knotted a loop at the end. "But hurry up. I think he's coming back!"

Christopher grabbed the makeshift lasso and aimed for the remote. Distant footsteps and a terrible giggle echoed up the stairwell. He had to be quick.

The loop landed just short of the bin.

"Quickly, try again," said Lauren. "Come on, concentrate!"

"Will you be quiet!" snapped Christopher. "You're not making this any easier."

The footsteps got louder.

Christopher threw again, and this time the loop landed on the remote.

"Brilliant," said Lauren. "Now just reel it in…"

Christopher pulled ever so gently, but the scarf slid silently over the remote and then fell to the floor. He'd have to try again … if he had time.

"Yoo-hoo!" Doctor Skinner's cry was close, nearly at the top of the stairs. "Who wants to make history?"

Christopher didn't stop to aim; he just threw the lasso and hoped. The loop snagged over the antenna.

"Hello, my little ones! Is everyone as excited as me?" As Doctor Skinner burst through the door Christopher tugged on the scarf and the remote control clattered to the floor.

"Now, let's get this set up." Skinner set down the large security eyeball he was carrying and began to connect its various wires to a recording device. Christopher stretched his arm out across the laboratory tiles.

"I really should have thought of this earlier," chuckled the doctor.

Christopher whipped the control through the bars and thrust it into his coat.

Skinner turned to them with eyes ablaze. "Who's ready for the grand finale?"

There is Always a Choice

"Where is your father now?" said Little Big Nose, a bead of sweat running down his nostril.

The blade of the scalpel hovered above the nose's tip.

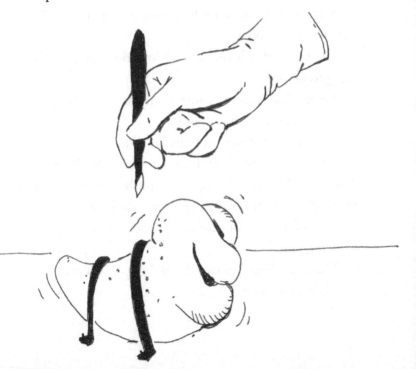

"I don't know ... he didn't say where he was going."

"And you haven't seen him since?"

"No, I have not!" Doctor Skinner prepared to make the first cut. "Now be quiet!"

Christopher was struggling with Scuttler's controls. The hand weaved across the floor of the laboratory, stumbling and skittering this way and that. Christopher had lots of experience with remote control cars but this was something else.

"Over there." Lauren pointed to a corner of the laboratory. "That's where he put them." By a dormant Funky Feet and a pile of old specimens, the keys to the cage hung from a low hook.

"Hurry up..." said Lauren. "He's about to start cutting."

Scuttler teetered on his fingertips and then clumsily crawled over to the keys.

"Now," said Christopher. "How do I make this thing reach up?"

He fiddled with the controls and stuck his tongue out of the corner of his mouth.

Scuttler sank down on to its knuckles.

"No, wrong way," said Christopher. "So if that's down ... this must be up." He pushed a lever and Scuttler's index finger stretched towards the keys.

"That's it," he whispered. "Quite easy once you get the hang of it."

The index finger quivered, reaching ... reaching.

"Just a bit more."

Then the finger suddenly flopped down, all power gone. Scuttler trembled and then collapsed in a limp pile on the floor.

"And why did your father leave?" asked the nose as he trembled in his straps.

"Because he was a coward," snarled Skinner and drew his hand across his brow.

"I don't understand," said Little Big Nose.

"I don't understand," whispered Christopher. "The controls are still working but Scuttler just isn't responding."

"It must be out of range," said Lauren. "You've got to get closer."

"He left because…" said Doctor Skinner and faltered. A sad look passed across his face. "He left because he knew my mother … he knew my mother was dying and he didn't want to watch."

The sad look changed into a scowl, "Happy now?"

"How old were you?"

"Eleven, twelve. I was young."

"So you looked after her as she died."

"Yes…"

"That was a very brave and kind thing to do."

"I had no choice," said Skinner.

"There is always a choice," replied the nose.

"Not for me there wasn't." The doctor narrowed his eyes and looked closely at the nose. "Now … if you don't mind I would like to get on."

He lowered the scalpel and Little Big Nose shuddered as the cold metal touched his skin.

"When my mother died," said the nose. "I couldn't help her at all."

Doctor Skinner raised the scalpel. "So, you of all noses should understand why I need to do this." His eyes sparkled with emotion and his hand shook. "If I could find out the secret of life … I could destroy death."

Doctor Skinner braced himself and prepared to make the cut. "Because of this sacrifice, no child need ever watch their mother die again."

"If you take away death, you change life," said Little Big Nose. "Every trail must have a beginning and an end. That's what makes life such an incredible experience."

"But it's horrible and mean and unfair. And … and …" The doctor's voice trembled. "It's sad … yes, that's it. Above all else … it's … sad."

"Yes … but its also beautiful," said the nose. "And it's the sadness that makes it so."

Little Big Nose spoke softly, "I know you miss your mother, I miss mine. But we can't bring them back…"

"But why?" whispered the doctor. "Why should it be this way?"

Christopher squeezed the control through the bars, held it at arm's length and frantically pushed the levers and switches. Scuttler's fingers twitched and once again stretched upwards.

Lauren peered over at the dissection table. "He's about to start cutting. We'll never get the keys back in time."

"I think," said Christopher. "That I have another idea."

"I have to do this," said Skinner. "For science, for my mother."

"But you made me," said the nose. "Please…"

"I'm sorry…" said Skinner.

Boogying Around the Laboratory

Skinner lifted the scalpel and looked around the laboratory. "What's that?"

A bass drum and cymbal.

Dum tusch tusch tisch tusch tusch tisch, dum dum tusch tisch tisch.

"What in the blazes?" cried Skinner.

Christopher smiled. "Cool daddy-o!"

The drum beat skittered along at its laidback pace and was joined by a single trumpet, which weaved a playful melody around the hypnotic rhythm. A double bass thrummed into the fray, giving the tune a deep and solid feel. Each instrument would solo and then give way to the next that would play, slowly building until the drums rolled, cymbals crashed and chimed, the bass went double time and the trumpet screamed at a high and frantic pitch and Funky Feet clicked its heels and was away: skipping, jiving and swaying. Boogying around the laboratory.

As Doctor Skinner glared at the dancing legs, Christopher made Scuttler crawl quickly under the dissection table and then whipped the controls behind his back.

"Most unusual," said the doctor, narrowing his eyes. "Machines don't just start by themselves." He shot Christopher and Lauren a look, but they just smiled back sweetly.

"Faulty circuitry?" said Christopher.

"Bad workmanship!" added Lauren.

The doctor scowled and cracked his twelve knuckles.

"This is only a minor setback!" he declared to the children. "It won't take long to deal with this contraption."

Funky Feet shimmied over to Lauren and Christopher and elegantly swirled around the cage. The doctor advanced upon the machine, the blood rising in his cheeks.

"I'm gonna give your shins such a kicking."

Lauren watched the machine intently. As Funky Feet reeled around the front of the cage, she very quickly reached out and flicked the speed dial up a notch.

It was a masterstroke. The record got faster and so did Funky Feet. Doctor Skinner lunged for the machine but it was off and away, dancing crazily about to a jazz tune that sounded as if it had been recorded by a band of hyperactive chipmunks.

Christopher clapped his hands in delight.

"Lauren! You're a genius!"

"You're a pain in the neck!" growled Skinner and chased after the frantic legs. Christopher and Lauren watched as Funky Feet out-jigged and out-jived the stumbling doctor. The machine was hard enough to control normally, but now it was on super speed it was unstoppable. The needle skipped and the machine's movements became even more erratic and uncontrollable.

"This is the absolute limit!" the doctor yelled as Funky Feet jitterbugged furiously around him. It was almost as if the machine were making fun of him. "Right, that's it!"

With a roar he threw himself upon the contraption just as the legs were beginning an ultra fast version of the high kicking can-can.

Thwack, smack, crack! Funky Feet's heels smashed Skinner's chin with three swift blows.

"That looked like it hurt," said Christopher.

The doctor's six knees gave way and he collapsed backwards, sending specimen jars crashing to the floor. Reaching out to steady himself, he grabbed onto the centrifuge, knocking its power button on as he did so.

With a shake of his head Doctor Skinner quickly regained his composure and, as the centrifuge hummed into life, he launched himself back at the swooning, sweeping, knee-bending, toe-flinging legs of funk.

"Christopher, now's the time."

Christopher looked down at the controls and focused. Scuttler sat just under the dissection table. He had to get the hand up there and free Little Big Nose. He could get the keys to their cage next, he just wanted to see his friend out of those straps. He pushed the remote back out through the bars so he would be in range, and fiddled with the levers and buttons.

The hand reached up, grabbed one of the dissection table legs and inched itself upwards.

"This isn't so hard once you get the hang of it," whispered Christopher as the hand crawled up the leg.

"You stupid knock-kneed disaster!" roared Doctor Skinner. "Come here!"

It was hard to tell who was causing more destruction around the laboratory – Funky Feet as it wobbled, kicked and hip swiveled or the doctor as he chased after it with his gangly arms and legs.

Computer screens splintered and cracked as elbows

and knees smashed into them, chairs went flying, the centrifuge span and span and all around glass, blue liquid and body parts lay everywhere.

All the while Doctor Skinner raged and cursed and Funky Feet played a ridiculous soundtrack of extra high speed jumping jazz.

Lauren tore her eyes away from the spectacle to check on Christopher's progress.

Scuttler swung deftly onto the table and fingertipped over to the trembling nose. Christopher pressed a button and the hand reached out and grappled with the thick leather straps.

"Well done," said Lauren. "You've really got the hang of it now."

Suddenly silence fell upon the laboratory.

The song had finished on the record and Funky Feet came to a standstill.

Christopher and Scuttler froze.

Doctor Skinner crept toward the record player.

"I've got you now, you pesky…" He lunged but it was too late. The next song came up and the legs were off again in a rapid jive.

"Aaarghhh … if I … when I … you're gonna be so…" Skinner skidded on an ear and flew backwards into the air, landing on the floor with a bone shuddering thud.

Christopher concentrated and fiddled. One strap was off.

Little Big Nose wasn't sure what to make of the whole thing. Whoever or whatever this hand was, he was just glad that it seemed to want to help. Soon he would be free.

"We've done it," said Lauren.

"Well, almost," replied Christopher.

The nose flared his nostrils and sighed with relief.

"Oh no you don't." Doctor Skinner rose from beneath the table and before Christopher could put Scuttler in reverse, he grabbed the hand.

"Well, well, well," he snarled. "My own invention has turned against me. What a terrible cliché! And you…" he turned on the nose. "All the time you were keeping me talking, you were plotting against me."

"I meant everything I said," replied the nose.

"A likely tale, or trail if you will … yes … a trail of deceit! That's what it was!"

"Leave him alone," yelled Lauren. "What do you expect if you lock children and noses up against their will?"

"Do be quiet, you insufferable little brat," shouted Skinner over Funky Feet's superfast soundtrack. "Though I have to say you two aren't as dumb as you look. Using Scuttler like that," he held the hand up. "Very ingenious!"

Christopher seized his chance. With a flick of a switch Scuttler's fingers and thumb formed a pincer. A pincer that grabbed Doctor Skinner's nose very hard.

"OW!" yelped Skinner and pulled at the hand. Christopher held the switch in position; he knew from bitter experience that Scuttler's grasp was strong and immovable.

"Ged id orf! Ged id orf!"

"Let the nose go!"

"Dever!" cried the doctor. His eyes crossed and his face turned a terrible purple.

"Then I guess you won't have a nose yourself!" Christopher tightened the grip. "That's the deal then is it? A nose for a nose!"

The doctor yanked and pulled at the hand but it wouldn't budge. Tears began to stream down his cheeks.

"Okay okay," he squealed.

Funky Feet almost seemed to jig in celebration as it swiveled around Lauren and Christopher's cage.

The Doctor fumbled with the last strap.

"Please jusd ged dis ding off. I cand breed!"

"Only when the nose is free, then I'll…" Christopher was silenced mid sentence as Funky Feet kicked up and knocked the control from his hands and high into the air.

Lauren watched the remote fly and reached out to catch it.

It landed just inches from her fingers and smashed into tiny little pieces.

"Oh no," she muttered.

Funky Feet jived on, oblivious.

Christopher and Lauren looked up at the doctor. He was already smiling. Scuttler slid from his face and landed on the floor with a lifeless thud. Funky Feet suddenly stopped as the high-speed jazz came to an abrupt end.

The doctor strolled over to the record player.

"End of side one," he said, reaching across and turning the machine off. A deadly quiet settled upon the laboratory. All that could be heard was the spinning of the centrifuge and Little Big Nose's wheezes.

Doctor Skinner calmly walked back to the dissection table.

"Right, now all that shenanigans is out of the way," he said picking up the scalpel. "I would like to continue with my research."

Mucus and the Moon

Christopher couldn't watch. Lauren put her arm around him and he buried his head in her shoulder.

"Leave him alone, you horrible man!" Her eyes

were red and angry with tears. "What has he done to you?"

Doctor Skinner stood over Little Big Nose and lit a candle. As he reached for his scalpel his face was a mask of shadows.

"He just betrayed me," said Skinner, looking from Lauren to the nose. "You pretended you were interested. Pretended to care about where your trail began … and all the while you were just buying time."

"No," said Little Big Nose. "That's not true."

Christopher looked up. Little Big Nose sounded utterly beaten, as if he were preparing for his fate.

"After all…" said the nose. "You are my father."

Christopher shook his head and tears rolled down his cheeks.

For a moment Doctor Skinner said nothing. "I am your creator, not your father. They are two completely different things."

"You are where my trail begins."

The doctor blinked and looked hard at the nose.

"Lies," he said finally. "You're just trying to confuse me."

"You are my father," continued the nose. "And I know in your heart you can be good."

The doctor's eyes glistened and the scalpel shook above the nose. He stumbled for the right words. "I don't want to be a father…"

"But you are…" said the nose.

"But I don't want to be … it's too confusing." The

doctor loosened his grip on the knife. "I need time to think…"

He looked at Little Big Nose with desperate eyes. "I don't know how to do the right thing…"

"Christopher? Lauren?" A cry came up the stairs and the door swung open.

"Dad!" cried Lauren.

"What is going on?" Mr Postlethwaite surveyed the room with furious eyes, seeing his children in a cage, human body parts on the floor. Then he saw the strange man with wild eyes.

Doctor Skinner raised his hands. "Listen," he said. "I can explain…"

Mr Postlethwaite grabbed him by the lapels.

Mrs Postlethwaite burst through the door. "Christopher, Lauren, you're all right!" In an instant she was at the cage.

"Where are the keys?" snarled Mr Postlethwaite.

Skinner held out a trembling finger. "The … there…"

Mr Postlethwaite pushed Skinner away, grabbed the keys and threw them to Christopher and Lauren's mum. She unlocked the door and the children rushed into her arms.

The doctor tried his best smile. "Excuse me, sir… but this has all been a terrible misunderstanding … I'm sure…"

Mr Postlethwaite stepped forward, pulled back his fist and thumped Doctor Skinner right on the nose. The doctor stumbled a few feet with a confused look on his face and then, with a tiny giggle, he teetered backwards across the laboratory. More specimen jars toppled from their shelves as the doctor's gangly arms spiraled helplessly, a table was knocked onto its side and the centrifuge slid to the floor. Skinner folded in on himself and collapsed in a corner.

Mr Postlethwaite inspected his knuckles, then looked over to his children.

"What is going on here?"

"Dad, watch out!" called Lauren.

Mr Postlethwaite stepped out of the centrifuge's path just in time. The machine was still working at full speed, but now it was dislodged, loose on the laboratory floor. Like a spinning top filled with snot it span around and around on the tiles. Sparks crackled across the darkened room and the beakers and test tubes of mucus rattled angrily.

The doctor rose unsteadily to his feet and looked around with bleary eyes. To him the centrifuge's spinning was a smudged and confusing spectacle. He blinked hard but still couldn't focus. Then there was a popping noise and a streak of green jumped from the machine and headed straight for him.

The beaker of snot smashed against the doctor's forehead with incredible force. Goo sprayed everywhere and Skinner fell back into his corner.

"Duck!" shouted Christopher. Mr Postlethwaite hit the floor. Lauren and Christopher huddled up to their mum.

Suddenly the laboratory was filled with flying mucus

and exploding glass. Like a strange fireworks display, the jars whizzed from the centrifuge and smashed against walls and ceilings. Lauren and Chrsitopher were held close to Mrs Postlethwaite's chest as snot and shards of glass showered down on them. Christopher was surrounded by the zipping sounds of airborne test tubes, mighty crashes and wet splats. He sneaked a look out from under his mother's arm. A thin spray of goo filled the air. Snot was everywhere. Over the walls, over his family and over the specimens that littered the floor.

The last candle fizzled out as a huge splodge of mucus dripped from the ceiling and onto its flame.

Darkness fell. The centrifuge slowly came to a halt.

Christopher looked across at his sister. He could just make out her shining goo-covered glasses.

"What's going on?" she said. "I can't see anything."

"What is this stuff?" said Mrs Postlethwaite.

Christopher opened his mouth to tell her, but a giggle popped out instead.

"What's funny?" said him mum.

Christopher tried again but it was no good, he was laughing too hard. Lauren heard his snickering in the darkness and soon her shoulders were shaking too.

Mrs Postlethwaite looked down in bemusement.

"Come on, what are you laughing at?"

Neither Christopher nor Lauren could say anything anymore. They held their sides and laughed and laughed and laughed.

"Everybody in one piece?" It was Mr Postlethwaite, calling through the darkness.

"I think so…" Mrs Postlethwaite inspected her children. "Are you okay?"

"I'll live" said Christopher.

"Just about…" added Lauren

Mr Postlethwaite clattered into an upended chair. "I wish I could see where I was going."

And as if by his request, the laboratory was suddenly filled with a pale yellow light.

All the Postlethwaites looked up and there, beyond the glass dome roof, in a gap between clouds, was the full moon.

"Just look at that," whispered Mrs Postlethwaite. "It's quite a view." She hugged her children a little closer.

"It's beautiful," said Little Big Nose. He had wriggled free of the last strap and was sitting on the edge of the table.

"Who said that?" whispered Mrs Postlethwaite.

"A friend," replied Christopher.

He looked across at his sister, who smiled back at him.

At first Christopher thought what he was seeing was just a trick of the light.

Lauren had flecks of sparkling green in her hair.

"What?" said Lauren seeing the expression on his face. "What is it?"

"Did you put glitter on today or something?"

"No" replied Lauren. She rubbed her glasses and peered closely at him. "Did you?"

He glanced down at his hands and saw that he was sparkling too. He reached across and wiped a big lump of green glow from Lauren's cheek.

It squished between his fingers.

"It's the snot," he said. "Something's happening to the snot."

Christopher looked around the laboratory. Everything was aglow.

A cloud skittered over the moon's face and for a second the glowing stopped. Then the cloud blustered away and once again the laboratory was engulfed in the incredible green light.

Christopher gazed around in wonder, a strange feeling washing over him.

"Do you feel that?" he said to Lauren.

His sister put her hand to her chest. "Yeah, I think so."

It felt like … she couldn't quite name it. It was the feeling you get when a song sends shivers down your spine, or the feeling of seeing somebody you love after a long time, or when you look out on a night's starry sky and you feel small and frightened but alive and excited all at the same moment. It was all these emotions and more. Her head and heart were awash with them.

Little Big Nose tingled all over with the strange sensation. It felt completely new but familiar as well. As the feeling grew he knew what he had to do. He flared his nostrils and began to hum.

Doctor Skinner couldn't believe what he was seeing and feeling. He too, like everyone in the room, felt the strange delicious ache and it was too much for him. It had been so long since he'd felt anything but loneliness and anger. He buried his head in his hands and wept.

Little Big Nose continued to hum as he sparkled in the moonlight. The song was his favourite of all slug tunes. It was a song that was used to call the herd together on happy occasions. It had a wonderful melody, filled with longing and hope.

Beneath him things began to move. For a moment it seemed as if the floor itself was squirming and twitching.

Glowing green fingers stretched, toes wriggled and a thousand tiny BURPs puckered up.

All the Postlethawites gasped as an eyeball rolled across the floor.

Every specimen, in its own time and own way, began to creep towards the centre of the room. A foot dragged itself by its toes. Two ears flipped and popped across the tiles like jumping beans. A mouth wriggled along like a caterpillar and a hand raised itself onto its fingertips and crawled over to a leg of the dissection table.

Using its BURPs the eyeball slurped itself onto the hand's back and then, looking very similar to Scuttler, the hand and the eye made their way up to Little Big Nose.

"What are they going to do to him?" said Lauren getting to her feet.

Christopher looked at the nose, who still sat happily humming to himself and the specimens.

"It's okay." He smiled at his sister and mother and then called over to his father. "It's okay Dad, everything's going to be just fine. Don't do anything."

"This is a very odd day," mumbled Mr Postlethwaite.

Christopher just hoped he was right. He looked back to the table. Little Big Nose was surrounded by wriggling body parts.

It was hard to see what was going on. The slug song floated through the air and was joined by the gentle squelching of countless BURPs.

The specimens writhed and crawled around the nose, a mass of limbs and flesh.

A swathe of clouds rushed across the sky and once again the laboratory was cast into darkness.

Fathers and Sons

Mr Postlethwaite lit the second candle and raised a warning finger toward Skinner.

"Stay where you are!"

The doctor shrunk back into his corner, his eyes never leaving the centre of the room.

"I don't believe it," whispered Lauren.

"It's incredible," said the doctor.

Everybody looked toward the dissection table with quiet awe. None of the crawling specimens remained. In their place was a boy.

Christopher's heart hammered against his chest.

"It can't be…" he said as he took a few small steps toward the sleeping child.

"Be careful…" said Mrs Postlethwaite.

"It's all right, Mum." Christopher looked at the boy's face. All in all a very normal looking face apart from the nose … that was rather large and was speckled by ginger freckles. "As I said … he's a friend."

He leant down and whispered in the boy's ear, "Little Big Nose … wake up … wake up."

The eyelids fluttered and then slowly opened. The boy gazed at Christopher with clever, gentle eyes.

A huge grin spread across Christopher's face.

"How do you feel?" he asked.

The boy thought for some time and then used his new voice for the first time.

"Complete," he said.

Christopher watched his dad wrap his big coat around the boy, and once again felt the tender ache in his chest. He looked down at his hands, but the goo wasn't glowing anymore. This feeling was his. It came straight from his heart.

He shyly sidled up to his father. Mr Postlethwaite was kneeling down and using a hanky to clear the remaining snot from the boy's face.

"What happened here?" he asked the boy.

Christopher rested his hand on his dad's shoulder.

"It's a long story," he said.

Mr Postlethwaite turned to his son.

"Hello, Chris..." He raised his hand to stroke Christopher's cheek but then stopped himself. He glanced around distractedly and then returned his gaze to his son.

"You know what?" he said. "I don't care what happened." He looked Christopher up and down. "All I care about is that you and your sister are safe... and that..." he stared deep into Christopher's eyes. "And that we can be friends again..."

Christopher looked down at his kneeling father and knew in an instant how much he had missed him in the last year. Tears welled in his eyes and he threw his arms around his dad. Mr Postlethwaite hugged Christopher tightly and rose to his feet, swinging the boy around him.

"Whoa," he said. "You're not getting any lighter." A single tear dropped down his cheek. "I was so worried. I'm so glad we found you."

"How did you find us?" asked Christopher as his dad put him down. "How did you know we were gone?"

"I check on you most nights," said Mrs Postlethwaite, who was busy hugging Lauren. "I wake up and can't get back to sleep unless I know you're safely tucked up in bed."

"And when your mum found your beds empty she phoned me…" said Mr Postlethwaite.

"And the rest was easy," added Mrs Postlethwaite.

"We just followed your footprints," said Mr Postlethwaite. "In the snow."

The boy on the table sneezed loudly and Christopher saw that he was shivering.

Mr Postlethwaite walked over to the boy and with one brisk movement scooped him up into his arms.

"Come on, let's get out of here. This young lad needs a hot bath and a bowl of soup." He shot a warning look at Doctor Skinner, who still lay sat crumpled and defeated in the corner.

"And you!" he growled. "This should really be a matter for the police … but I have no idea what to tell them, and I doubt they'd believe a word of it." He lowered his voice ominously. "But I'm telling you now … if you go anywhere near any of these children ever again…"

Mrs Postlethwaite took his arm. "Come on, let's go."

"Wait!" The boy sprung from Mr Postlethwaite's arms and limped across the laboratory. "My friends…"

He reached up onto a shelf and pulled down a jar. He inspected it closely and then for the first time, his eyes stung with tears.

"They didn't have any air" he said quietly to himself. Christopher walked across to his friend and rested his arm on his shoulder. The slugs lay in a lifeless pile.

"Come on, Little Big Nose," he said. "Let's take you home."

"Erm ... before you go. I was wondering..." Doctor Skinner stumbled awkwardly to his feet.

Mr Postlethwaite stepped forward. "I've warned you."

The doctor held up his hands. "I want to help..." he said meekly. "Truly..." He looked to the boy and back at Mr Postlethwaite. "I would like to help."

Doctor Skinner smiled. It wasn't his usual forty-tooth grin, but a shy helpless smile. He twiddled his twelve fingers and searched to find the right words.

"Something happened ..." he began. "Something happened ... I felt it ... we all saw it." He gestured around the laboratory with his long arms.

"Something happened ... and I don't know if it was science or ... or ... magic." He winced at the word. "But I think I understand it."

He looked up to the night sky. A small break in the clouds was appearing.

"Please," said Doctor Skinner holding out his hand for the jar of slugs. "We have to be quick."

The doctor pulled out the last intact test tube of snot from the safety of his pocket. He unscrewed the cork and poured the contents over the lifeless slugs that now lay on the dissection table.

"Now all we have to do is wait..."

The gap in the clouds grew and the full moon

peaked through. The slugs began to sparkle a rich damp green.

Doctor Skinner's eyes shone with the light of new discovery.

"The full moon… " he said eagerly. "The full moon was the missing ingredient."

The slugs' antennae twitched to life and rose into the air like fresh spring shoots searching for the sun.

The boy watched the waking slugs and the look of excitement on the doctor's face.

"A full moon's child is touched by magic…" he said. "You said it was magic."

The doctor's cheeks flushed. "I said … I said … I didn't know what it was…"

He turned to look at the boy with searching eyes.

"But whatever it was … it created something far more incredible than all my contraptions thrown together."

The boy returned the doctor's serious gaze and then smiled. "It's changed you," he said, almost in a whisper.

"Not changed," said the doctor quietly. "Maybe … opened my eyes … it's hard to describe … I felt things … things I haven't felt for years."

"And what did you feel?"

"Alone."

The boy stepped forward and rested a hand on the doctor's arm.

"If you like, I could come and visit you … keep you company."

"I would like that…" said Doctor Skinner.

"I think you were right," said the boy, "you are not my father."

Like eyelashes over a shining eye, the clouds once again swept across the moon.

"But in time…" said the boy, "I think maybe you could be."

The New World

"David … David!" Lauren waved and jumped in the snow. "Over here."

Christopher watched the dark-haired boy approaching and said the name to himself, under his breath.

"David…" It was two weeks since that night at Doctor Skinner's mansion. Little Big Nose, the boy,

had renamed himself on the walk home. And yet Christopher still couldn't quite get used to it.

Lauren watched David approach and felt the familiar butterflies in her stomach. She decided she liked his eyes best of all. They were sky blue and old beyond their years. They were smart eyes, but soft too. Thoughtful. Second best was his nose. True, it was pretty big, but Lauren thought it made him look very serious and noble. Like a Shakespearean actor or a Greek God.

He smiled at her and her freckled cheeks blushed.

"Are you going to see your dad?" he asked.

"Yeah," said Christopher eagerly. "We're going to make snow men. Well, to be exact … snow ogres."

David laughed.

"How's the doctor?" said Lauren.

"Okay," said David with a little wince. "Very quiet." He thrust his hands into his pockets. "Though he did create something truly terrible the other day…"

"Oh no…" groaned Christopher. "What now?"

"Omelette" grinned David. "He tried to cook me an omelette." He wrinkled up his nose. "It was horrible … still soft and runny in the middle. A bit like snot."

They laughed and looked out on the white fields and frosted trees. David lifted his large nose to the air and sniffed deeply.

"Snow always smells so fresh and clean to me," he said. "It makes me think of new beginnings."

Christopher gazed around at the brilliant crystal

landscape. His friend was right, the world did look new as it shone and glistened, wearing its bright white winter coat.

"You know what it makes me think of?" said Christopher, reaching down. "Snowball fights!" he shouted and thrust a handful down David's neck.

"Oooh, it's freezing" cried David, wriggling, as Christopher ran off down the hill laughing.

Lauren smirked at David. "Shall we get him?"

"I think we should," replied David.

Lauren and David sped after Christopher, laughing and throwing snowballs through the crisp air.

As the children disappeared into the woods, the hill fell silent.

Once again the world was fresh, quiet and new. The only sign of life were three pairs of footprints, sunk deep into the sparkling snow.

If, later that day, you were to stumble upon these footprints and decide it might be fun to follow them, through the woods and over the hills, through the bright clean snow, you might find that they could tell a story.

You would see that sometimes a pair would run ahead and then turn suddenly (you might guess) to send a snowball whizzing through the air.

Other times you might frown and smile as you try to follow the footprints in and out of the trees, their paths crossing and zigzagging in and around each other so many times that it becomes impossible to tell one from the other.

But mostly, if you were to follow these footprints, these trails, left by Lauren, Christopher and David in the shining white snow, you would notice that, more often than not ... they were together.